CW00448566

VAMPIRE

BRIDES

TO HAVE AND TO HOLD

A Novel by

Yvonne Robertson

Copyright 2019 © Yvonne Robertson

Published by Major Key Publishing, LLC

www.majorkeypublishing.com

ALL RIGHTS RESERVED.

Any unauthorized reprint or use of the material is prohibited. No part of this book may be reproduced or transmitted in any form or by any means, electronic, or mechanical, including photocopying, recording, or by any information storage without express permission by the publisher.

This is an original work of fiction. Names, characters, places and incidents are either products of the author's imagination or are used fictitiously and any resemblance to actual persons, living or dead is entirely coincidental.

Contains explicit language & adult themes suitable for ages 16+

To submit a manuscript for our review,

email us at

submissions@majorkeypublishing.com

To all of my friends (Old and new) and family who have supported and encouraged my continued writing. Thank you from the bottom of my pitifully romantic heart.

PROLOGUE

It is extremely rare for a vampire female to conceive a child. There has been a few in the history of our kind, but I personally suspect that the female was not a full blood vampire. Some of us, have in the past, mated with humans but sadly they are not strong enough to bear our young and it has always been strictly against our laws, that is until recently.

As I passed my five hundredth year on this earth I began to think constantly about the future of our House and about my heirs. I guess we are the equivalent of Vampire royalty and my son Luca, the eldest and heir apparent would be a capable, fair and just ruler.

We had all sworn a long time ago not to take the lives of any human unless they were on the brink of death, as was the case with his brothers. Luca, we made an exception for, as he would have been left in this world with no-one if we hadn't changed him too. He begged us to make him immortal.

The only way I could see the continuation of our house was for my sons to mate with hybrid humans. Women with mixed blood, elves, fae, lycan were all much stronger than their full human sisters and were capable of bearing our children. I finally got the backing of the vampire council, most of them anyway, and I began to plan.

My soulmate and life long partner, a witch in her previous life, began searching in earnest for the women destined to be with our sons for eternity, Violette loved our sons fiercely and wanted them to find love with their partners too. I thought that a rather tall order but I didn't really bet on my mates tenacity and her extreme powers...

Hendrik Van Buren.

CHAPTER ONE

Sierra

Sierra Adams sighed heavily and ran her fingers through her thick, blond hair as she regarded the ever-growing mountain of bills on the table in front of her. There was no possible way to stretch her meager salary to cover even a fraction of them and next month there would be another pile to add to these.

She ripped the sheet of paper from the pad, scrunched up the columns of figures in frustration and tossed it in the bin. The utilities she could live without at a push, at least until she had finished paying all of her Grandmas medical bills but she needed gas for her car and she still had to eat. Thankfully, working at a diner meant she could eat on the job, at least on the days when she was working.

She clicked off the hall light and wearily made her way upstairs to her bedroom. Tomorrow was her day off, she had volunteered to work the extra shift but Sal had insisted she stay home and put her feet up.

"You have worked every day straight for a month kid, stay home and take a break, please," she knew he meant it and bit off the argument forming on her lips when she saw the stern look on his face, but she really could have used the extra money, especially the generous tips from her regulars.

Pulling on a pair of cotton shorts and a tank top she brushed her teeth and hair and climbed into the oversized bed in the master that had once been Grandmas. She liked to imagine she could still smell the vanilla and sandalwood fragrance that had always surrounded the unorthodox, free-spirited woman but it was unlikely as it had been six months since she had passed away.

She had inherited this charming old house, the only home she had ever known, but there hadn't been any money left over after her illness and untimely death. She felt the all too familiar ache settle in her heart, her Grandma had been everything to her.

Rachel Adams had been the only constant presence in

her life and had raised Sierra since she was just a few days old. Her mother Vivienne, who Grandma said was wild and uncontrollable, had died a few months after she had left Sierra with Rachel and gone off with her latest beau. She had never known who her father was and Grandma didn't much like to talk about Vivienne.

She suspected her mother had left her with her Grandma without as much as a backward glance and she found it hard to grieve for a woman she had never known. She looked at the photo on the bedside of the three of them, her as a newborn, her mother, petite and beautiful with wild black hair and her Grandma Rachel, her long dark blonde hair blowing on the breeze.

Grandpa had been behind the camera, but she didn't remember much about him either. Photos of them were scattered throughout the house but her memories of him were vague at best. Despite everything, she had always felt enveloped in love and warmth in this house.

She clicked off the light and hoped tomorrow would bring a solution, the only thing she had worth selling was this house and she needed to keep a roof over her head.

She tossed and turned restlessly before sleep finally claimed her in the early hours of the morning.

She dreamed of him again. He had been coming to her in her dreams every night for weeks now and she knew it was probably her subconscious playing tricks but she yearned for these interactions.

She hugged her pillow to her as he smoothed the hair back from her face and brushed his lips very lightly across hers. She inhaled the clean scent of shampoo, maybe a hint of cedarwood or pine and the rough sensation of stubble on her smooth cheek was almost tangible. She sighed with pleasure when he whispered endearments in her ear and her hands threaded into his hair. The heat was spreading through her body and she wanted him to kiss her properly, hold her in his arms, but he pulled back and kissed her hand instead before he disappeared.

Her eyes flew open as she bolted upright in bed and glanced quickly around the room, a laugh escaped her still tingling lips.

"I am going mad," she said aloud as she shook her

head, "The man of my dreams is nothing but a figment of my overactive imagination."

It was still very early but knowing sleep would evade her for the rest of the day she padded downstairs and put a pot of coffee on to brew. She liked to sit on the porch in the early mornings and she pulled the afghan from the back of the sofa and carried her cup outside to sit in Grandma's old rocker.

She heard a couple of cars in the distance but otherwise, the air was still and silent. The blanket wrapped around her body kept her warm and she rocked back and forth as she sipped the hot drink. She saw lights come on periodically in the other houses as people woke up to start their day.

She had grown up in this small town, lived here all of her young life and yet she never truly felt like she belonged here. Her mother had been a hellion and her legacy still lived on in the small town. Although her Grandma had been well enough liked, she knew some of the locals considered her to be a bit of a flake, with her potions and powders and her new age ideas but Sierra knew the real Rachel. She had been warm, loving and giving and she missed her terribly.

She waved to her new neighbor, Greer, as she passed by on the way to work. She had moved in a few weeks back and Sierra had been drawn to her. She didn't make friends too easily as she was naturally reticent but there was something about the tall willowy redhead that she liked very much and she seemed to feel the same way.

Greer Ashwood was a year older than her at twenty-three and worked at the local hospital as a nurse. She had rented a small, one story, two-bedroom house along the street from her. They had met at the diner and struck up a conversation and she had been to Greer's house for pizza last week. She pulled out her phone and sent her a text asking if she wanted to come over for dinner tonight, she could rustle up something decent from the contents of the freezer. She knew she wouldn't answer her now until she got to work.

She showered and dressed in softly faded jeans and a t-shirt and decided that today she would finalize the painful task of sorting through the remainder of Rachel's possessions. She had already donated her clothes to the local charity shop and a smile tugged at her lips at the thought of some of the townsfolk wearing her Grandmas brightly colored bohemian skirts and dresses.

Rachel had also made and sold beautiful, semi-precious jewelry, to supplement her retirement income and Sierra began unpacking those boxes first.

There was still a fair amount of stock left over and she thought she might try and sell them online. Rachel had mainly sold them at craft fairs around the county, but Sierra had a full-time job at the diner so Etsy or eBay was looking like a more viable prospect. She unpacked and displayed them to take pictures and uploaded them on her laptop.

She had always loved her Grandma's jewelry and kept a few of her favorite pieces back from the sale to keep as a memento of her. She stopped long enough to answer Greer's text, telling her to come around at seven, and to make a ham and tomato sandwich and a fresh pot of coffee. As she ate her lunch, she wandered around the house making a mental list of tasks, before she was forced to tackle the next stack of boxes.

There were two bedrooms and a bathroom upstairs, the living room, kitchen, dining room and another bathroom downstairs as well as Grandmas tiny office. She had already cleared it out and the papers she found were still in a box here somewhere. His heart swelled as she looked around her, she loved this little house, she had never known any other home.

She worked steadily making piles of things she could sell or donate and storing the things she wanted to keep in her bedroom closet. She kept the documents box for last, not really caring to look through Rachels most private things. She glanced around the bedroom she had slept in growing-up, before Rachel had passed away and she had taken over the master. It was now empty apart from the bed, a small dresser and a nightstand and she wondered briefly if she could rent out a room, it would certainly help to pay the bills.

She carried the heavy box containing her Grandmas papers downstairs to the kitchen dumping it on the table and washed her hands before going through the freezer and defrosting a pack of ground beef to make spaghetti for dinner. She skillfully chopped onions, tomatoes and garlic and put the sauce on to simmer. She set the garlic bread aside to defrost.

She was happy Greer was free to join her for dinner tonight. They would eat here in the kitchen, the dining room was very rarely used these days. She carefully put the receipts she had left out last night in the drawer with the calculator and her notepad.

Getting back on task, she opened the flaps on the cardboard box and started to sort through, discarding old receipts and setting aside photographs to keep. She packed her Grandmas will and the last few years of tax returns into a smaller empty box to store in the attic.

She was almost at the bottom of the box when she found a fairly new manilla envelope, still sealed but with no writing or other clues as to what it contained. She leaned back and furrowed her brow, how had she missed this, granted, the last time she had only given the papers a cursory glance before putting them back in the box to deal with later on, but she was quite sure this hadn't been there before.

She slipped her finger under the gum strip and tore open the flap to look inside. Her heart nearly jumped out of her chest when she saw the contents. It was stuffed full with money, mainly twenty and fifty dollar bills. She emptied the piles of used notes onto the table and her racing heart thumped loudly in her ears. She looked around as if someone might be watching before she started to count them and was shocked to find that there must be close to twenty-five thousand dollars in total. Her hands were shaking and she started to cry, the worries of the last few months eased away as she stared at the money.

Her Grandma must have been stashing this money for a long time. She had left everything to her in her will, there was no one else, so she guessed it now belonged to her. She had enough to clear the remaining medical and utility bills with a little bit left over. She only had a semester left at the local community college to get her degree in computer programming and she just had enough to cover the cost.

All of a sudden, her life started to look very differently to her and she said a silent thank you to her grandma as she packed the money away in the little safe in the tiny office off the kitchen. She was far from rich but she would be able to pay her bills if she budgeted very carefully.

She quickly showered and changed into clean jeans and a white cotton blouse, singing to herself as she set the table, Greer would be here in a few minutes and for the first time in ages she felt like celebrating, she hadn't felt this lighthearted in forever.

CHAPTER TWO

Luca

I knew tonight was the night. I was going to go inside the house and watch her while she slept. For many weeks now I had been invading her dreams, coaxing her to get to know me, to like me, to want me, but it also frustrated me beyond belief and I wanted to feel her skin beneath my touch and inhale her intoxicating scent up close. I knew there was little chance of being caught, I would sense her wakening long before she actually did.

I knew my parents and brothers would think me foolish for waiting so long but I didn't want to rush her and ruin everything and anyway, I cared not what anyone else thought.

When my father had told us of his desire to see us mated to women from worlds vastly different from ours we had thought he was joking at first. We rarely mated with the others as it was paramount that we keep our existence hidden from a world that would want to enslave or torture us just for being different. The elves, witches, lycan and fae all knew of our kind and we of theirs, but the humans were a different breed altogether. They had an inane need to kill whatever they didn't understand. They were so far behind the rest of us in all but technology and that in itself made them dangerous.

I did chuckle however when I read their fables and fairy stories about us, but the fact that they were so ill-informed did help to keep us hidden from them.

We don't sleep in coffins or exist only to seduce innocent young virgins and drain them of their blood, although my brother Finn has been known to seduce a few in his time. We don't necessarily need to have human blood to survive, we can also drink from other beings including other vampires, but it's human blood that makes us strongest and it's what we crave more than anything else. It's like dining on filet mignon compared to a hotdog. The taste of their blood is almost irresistible to us and in turn, our scent is intoxicating for them, a perfect weapon designed to draw them to us and gain their trust.

We do drink from humans, without their knowledge from time to time and without harm to them. Finn will dance close to a pretty girl in a club and run his tongue across her skin, numbing the area before he sneaks a few sips of her blood and seals the area again without her even realizing she's been bitten. My brother Aeric likes his victims intoxicated, which gives him a buzz when he drinks from them and they are usually too tipsy to realize that their date is feeding on them.

Ettore, however, is a bit of a snob and thinks that mating with a human is beneath him, he will drink from them of course and would never cause any harm, but he is at this time still furious with our father for laying these conditions on our mating. Father is the undisputed leader of our House and his word is law in our world. Ettore wants to choose his own mate and I had adamantly sided with him, at least at first, until I first laid eyes on my soul marked.

Father had spent many, many years researching what I first considered to be an experiment but he was convinced this was the way forward. The Vampire House of Van Buren would have to breed with females from the others, this was the only way to ensure our House would continue. Regardless of folklore, it is almost impossible for a vampire female to conceive. It's much less difficult for the males to reproduce however as they don't have the same changes in their bodies as they age and in the past human women had conceived through a liaison with our kind. Most didn't survive as humans don't have our strength to endure a hybrid pregnancy, but the rare ones that did survive and grow didn't age after they reached adulthood and this doesn't go unnoticed. Many hybrids were hunted and slaughtered, mainly through old wives tales and superstition. This last few hundred years, interbreeding has been outlawed...until now!

My father had the councils full backing and my brothers and I were sent out to observe the women identified by our mother as our life mates. All of them had been raised in the human world, although none of them were fully human, a fact which only made them stronger and with gifts of their own.

They all knew or at least suspected what they were,

except Sierra, she didn't know that her Grandfather had been Elven, or that she would become my immortal mate and the mother of my children.

Mother was a witch before she was changed and has the gift of foresight. Sierra Adams was the girl she saw in her dreams for me, her eldest and the heir apparent.

I was able to gain access to the house easily again and gently lowered myself onto the bed beside her as I watched her chest rise and fall. Her sweet scent empowered me as I touched a stray strand of her golden hair and brushed it from her face. I couldn't resist the impulse to kiss her and softly pressed my lips to hers. She parted them slightly and a soft moan escaped her and my stomach clenched with need. I wanted to gather her in my arms and bury myself in her sweet body so badly I could feel my fangs extending and I knew I had to have her soon.........or I might just go out of my mind.

I saw her breathing change and I quickly left, locking the door behind me and heading back to my family before she woke, deciding that tomorrow I would arrange to meet her for the first time. I couldn't yet hear her thoughts, but I could feel her emotions now, even from a few miles away and I sensed a calmness in her that hadn't been there before.

The money I had hidden in her Grandmother's things yesterday had the desired effect and had eased her troubled mind. I smiled like a kid as I thought about the day ahead.

CHAPTER THREE

Sierra

She told Greer about the money she had found
stashed among her Grandma's papers and her friend was
genuinely happy for her.

"Oh Sierra, I'm so pleased for you," she said as she
sipped on her wine. "I know how worried you've been
finding the money for all the medical bills that have been
building up."

They hadn't known each other for very long but
Sierra felt an affinity with her and trusted her as if she
had known her for years and they had already confided
many things to each other. Like her, Greer's parents were
gone and she was also an only child. She felt a bond, a
rapport with her. Greer was the closest to a best friend
Sierra had ever had.

She topped up their glasses from the bottle of rose
Greer brought with her and they went outside and sat on

the porch to watch the sun go down. She loved being outside and barring extremely cold weather, would sit out here most days to unwind after work.

She told her friend she was also going to go back to school to finish her degree. She needed to speak to Sal to see if she could fit her shifts around her classes but she was sure he would be fine with it as long as she was flexible with her time. Greer told her she had a fair amount of student loans to pay back too but that it was the only way she could afford to go to school to become a nurse.

"I have been in foster care most of my life and out on my own since I was eighteen," she explained, "It will take me years to pay it all back but I make a decent salary and it will be paid back someday," she shrugged, clearly unconcerned and they watched the orange globe disappear on the horizon. They sat in companionable silence, although Sierra noticed her friend's eyes dart around as the light faded and she suddenly stood up and said she had to go home.

"Thanks again love," she hugged Sierra and arranged

to meet her again in a few days time for dinner at her house. She glanced around her again and Sierra asked if she was okay. She was quiet for quite some time and Sierra studied her friend's lovely face, her intelligent green eyes watchful and her long red hair blowing gently in the evening breeze. Eventually Greer lowered her voice and spoke again.

"Since I moved here, I have had the feeling that I am being watched," she stared off into the darkness, "Everywhere I go, sometimes even in the middle of the night," she said softly and Sierra felt a shiver run through her as her friend snapped out of her reverie and hugged her again,

"Probably just being silly, sorry Sierra, I didn't mean to scare you," she smiled but Sierra didn't smile back.

"Greer, I have felt it too," she said quietly, "But I'm not afraid, someone is watching me but they don't mean me any harm," she said with a conviction she couldn't possibly know.

She stood on the porch and watched her friend walk back to her own house, a little further down the street before she locked the house up securely as she had promised Greer she would.

She made some tea, sweetened with honey to take up to bed with her and sipped on it while she ran a bath and poured a generous amount of scented bath salts into the water. She stripped off her clothes and dumped them in the hamper before she stepped into the hot, rose-scented water.

She piled her honey blonde hair into a scrunchie and sighed as the hot water lapped around her soothing her body. She leaned back and closed her eyes and let her mind drift to her fantasy lover, she knew he would come to her in her dreams again tonight, he always did. She could feel his hands caressing her skin, his lips on hers or on the delicate skin on her neck and she shivered with delicious anticipation, she could almost feel his breath gently blowing across the nape of her neck.

The hairs stood up on her arms and she snapped open her eyes, scanning the bathroom and into the open door of the bedroom but everything looked just as she left it. That had felt so real, her skin tingled where she felt his breath.

She picked up the scented soap and washed her body, suddenly aware of her nakedness and she once again scanned the area around her but saw nothing amiss.

She drained the water away and wrapped a large towel around her and rubbed her skin until it was pink. She applied her favorite body lotion and brushed out her long hair, donning a pair of panties and a clean tank top before slipping under the smooth cotton sheets and the well washed handmade quilt.

It was fairly warm tonight and she sat up on the pillows, trying without success to read the same paragraph over and over again while she finished her tea. The feeling she had that she was being watched was stronger than ever and she eventually closed her book and turned out the bedside lamp. The streetlight shone through the crack in the curtain, casting an eerie glow over the room.

"I can feel your presence," she whispered into the dark and could have sworn she heard a faint chuckle in reply.

CHAPTER FOUR

Luca

'Clever girl', I thought with a smile. She could sense me around her and that was good. I thought it would take a lot longer for her to unlock the hidden gifts inside her and start to become what she was always destined to be.

I was startled when she opened her eyes while she was bathing last night and I was glad I was standing behind her or she may have seen something, not me, per se, as I could move much quicker than that, but she would have seen movement, a flash of color maybe and I didn't want to frighten her. I realized she would probably freak out if she knew I watched her when she was naked but our kind don't have the same hang-ups about our bodies as humans do.

Of course, I appreciated her naked form, she was stunning and I knew if she let me, I would become her adoring devotee. She could now sense when I was watching her and my general presence when I was near.

I had almost shown myself to her at the look in her beautiful violet eyes, fringed with dark lashes, her thick golden hair piled on top of her head, showing off her long neck and those full, sweet lips begging for me to kiss them.

She was the most gorgeous creature I had ever encountered in my two hundred plus years and soon she would be mine for eternity. I could feel my arousal at the thought of claiming her and knew I couldn't wait for much longer. She gave off such an air of innocence it was like an aphrodisiac and I surprised myself because I usually did not care about the past exploits of my lovers, that was a very human trait. In Sierra's case though I felt murderous at the thought of another touching or tasting her undeniable sweetness.

She certainly wasn't immune to me, her body's reaction to my touch, even in her dreams was very encouraging and I aimed to push her just a little further tonight.

I was, however, surprised to hear her friend Greer

voice her thoughts that she was being watched too. Greer was half-elf and sensed already what she was and despite being raised without a family to guide her, she had tapped into her gifts at a very young age. I knew she would probably be able to sense me so I had stayed back in the shadows when she was talking with Sierra on the porch, but I wasn't the one watching over her in the night which could only mean that my brother, Ettore, was. He clearly wasn't as indifferent to her as his future mate as he claimed to be. The thought brought a smile to my lips.

Mother had helped father to execute all of this months ago and she had arranged, by way of planting suggestion, for Greer to be hired at the local hospital recently and for her to find a house to rent close to Sierra. Mother felt it important that our mates have an affinity with each other and I had to agree. This was going to be the biggest shock imaginable for these women, especially Sierra as she didn't know she was anything other than fully human. The one thing mother couldn't control though was free will, only I could make Sierra want me as much as I wanted her but I was going to have to earn it the old-fashioned way.

In the vampire world, the heir to our House usually lives in their parent's home and bring their life partners to live there too. My brothers and I all have suites in our parent's house and it's expected that we will live there with our own families too.

The Van Buren House isn't really aptly named as it is something of a mansion, hidden deep in the woods and is part of an entire estate of around fifty or so homes, that house many vampires, elves and fae. The estate boasts a small medical clinic, a school and a blacksmiths workshop as well as the many family homes. We have extensive schooling and training for the youngsters but there are not too many of them and Erudussa is their teacher.

The estate has been glamoured to help it escape the notice of the humans that may happen to pass by and stumble upon it. I am hoping the elves that live on the estate and work for my father will help my new mate in understanding and teaching her the hidden gifts of the elven world within her.

Despite human folklore that we can't be outside in daylight, it was a lovely sunny day and I found my mother in the garden tending to her roses, it was one of her many passions. She stood and hugged me when I approached and I stifled a smile at the questioning eyes. She was no different from any other mother, apart from being almost five hundred years old, yet she looked to be in her mid-forties and just wanted to see her sons happy. She was still beautiful in an ethereal kind of way and was utterly adored by my father.

My brothers and I are full blood brothers and our mother found us at the battle of Borodino where Napoleon was forced to end his invasion of Russia after losing almost a third of his army. I was twenty-seven years old at the time, Ettore a year younger, the twins Finn and Ronan only twenty-four and Aeric, the baby was twenty-three.

I had stumbled across Ettore, bleeding heavily and near to death and I was desperate, at a loss what to do with him when she found us, drawn to the scent of his blood. I had no idea what she was until she showed me her fangs, her incredible speed and strength and in my mother's case, her use of a little magic, formerly being a witch before she was changed. Her name was Violette and she was nothing like the horror stories we had been told to frighten us as children.

She asked my brother for permission to save his life by changing him to be like her. Ettore had agreed quickly as the alternative was death. I left him with her and gone in search of our younger brothers Finn and Ronan who had also sustained fatal wounds and she saved them too.

None of us had known what had happened to Aeric, the baby of the family and when I told her about him as she sat with me by the fire, she held my hand in hers and chanted over and over to herself as she searched my mind for him and left as quickly as she had come, telling me my brothers change would be complete in a few days.

I watched over the three of them as they burned inside, feverish and incoherent, and on the third day, she came back. There was a man with her whom she said was her mate. A huge imposing figure with a kind face called Hendrick Van Buren and he had my little brother cradled in his arms. I knew he too was a vampire, a very old one and that Aeric would soon be one too. I was the only one of us still human.

That same night I asked Violette to change me as well as all that I held dear to me in the world was right here and I wanted to be with my brothers. She looked at me for the longest time and then she nodded, adding that it should be somewhat easier for me because I was healthy.

We have all been together ever since and although I love and honor my father dearly, I have always had a special bond with my mother, we all owe her everything that we are, over and above the bond of vampire and creator. Our parents have more humanity than almost everyone I have ever known.

We ate an early dinner together as my parents demanded at least once a week. Another fallacy perpetrated by humans that we don't eat food, we can and do eat but usually only once each day and I favor rare steak and red wine.

My father, a little impatiently, wanted to know how our plans were coming along and though I filled them in on the basics I refused to go in to intimate details with him, I was a grown man and my relationship with Sierra was off limits to him, but I did tell them that I thought it was time for Sierra to meet me in person and my mother nodded her approval.

I had to force my wayward heart to calm down as I thought about the night ahead.

CHAPTER FIVE

Sierra

The diner was incredibly busy today and she was glad
of the pocketful of tips but her feet ached and she was
glad when she looked at the clock, she only had about
twenty minutes left of her shift. The door chimed and
Brynna, the young waitress that had started working there
just last week, called out to her.

"Single at your table, Sierra."

She called back her thanks and took her pen and
notepad from the pocket of her starched white apron to
serve her last customer of the day.

As she approached the table, she felt a tingle run
down her spine and the woodsy, spicy smell that tickled
her senses was so familiar yet…

"What can I get you," she asked the dark-haired, well-
dressed man with his head buried in the menu. She could
tell at a glance that the impeccably tailored suit jacket

probably cost more than her car.

"Just coffee please," he answered in a deep pleasant timbre and as he lifted his head, she took a step back as she stared into the face of the man who, for many weeks, had invaded her mind, body and soul as he haunted her dreams.

The granite, stubbled jaw line, the thick, dark hair that brushed his collar and azure eyes, as blue as the sky on a hot summer's day. She drank in his smell and felt herself inexplicably lean towards him, unable to break his gaze. Heat pooled in her stomach and she had to breathe deeply to calm her wayward heart. She saw the slow, lazy smile that crossed his features as he watched her knowingly and the gleam of dazzling white teeth as his full lips parted and he gave her the full wattage of his smile.

The heat radiated through her entire body, from her toes to her ever-reddening cheeks. She shook her head to clear her brain and turned on her heel to get his coffee. She heard his low chuckle as she walked away and had such a feeling of deja vu.

"Wow," Brynna whispered behind her, "What. A.

Babe."

She rolled her eyes at the other waitress and carried the full pot back to his table. Her hand shook as she poured and he reached out and took her free hand, running his thumb slowly over her palm. She swallowed before she spoke again but didn't pull her hand away immediately as the familiarity of his touch was soothing to her.

"Can I get you anything else," she met his eyes and a jolt went through her at the pull she felt from their piercing blue depths.

"No thank you Sierra, not just yet," he smiled again and leaned back in his chair to watch her as she refilled coffee and wiped down tables.

She wore a name badge at work so that was no surprise, but the way he said her name had her skin break out in goosebumps. Having him here, watching her was very disconcerting but she was magnetically drawn to him and didn't want to resist the involuntary tug towards him whenever she got close.

She glanced his way again and found the table empty

and heaved a sigh. What the heck, she felt relieved and bereft at the same time and why was she having heavy dreams about this guy, he must have been in here before, but somehow knew that wasn't so, she would have remembered him in a heartbeat.

She picked up his check and realized he had left the money for his coffee and a hundred-dollar bill on the table as a tip, she stared at it and Brynna whistled and grinned. She tucked the bill into her pocket and put the coffee money in the register. Taking off her apron she called goodbye to Sal and Brynna and the door chimed on her way out.

She looked around her and locked her car doors when she climbed in, the feeling of being watched was much stronger tonight. She couldn't explain how, but she knew that she wasn't in danger. She glanced in her mirror several times, but there was nothing behind her the entire way home.

She had been avoiding thinking about the guy in the diner but he invaded her mind now that she was alone. He was utterly gorgeous and sexy but it was more than that, much more, and she knew she would give anything just to see him again, to lose herself in the depths of those amazing blue eyes and feel those lips on her tingling skin.

CHAPTER SIX

Luca

Feeling Sierra's emotions as she spoke to me in the diner gave me a great deal of hope. The first thing I felt from her was shock, then happiness and then her arousal, her pupils dilated, her breathing became a little labored and her eyes were fixed on my lips before she even uttered a word. When she finally looked in my eyes, I saw the same feelings, I harbored, reflected there and my heart soared.

I felt my own heightened state as she stood beside me and I took a chance when I touched her hand but she didn't pull away from me. It took every ounce of strength I could muster to walk away from her. I must reveal myself, go to her tonight and tell her who I am.

Like most of my kind, my eyesight is very acute and I watched her from the highest branches of the tree in her backyard. I waited until she had climbed into bed before I jumped down and unlocked her door, with a little basic magic my mother taught me. I explored the ground floor of her house while I waited for her to fall asleep. I heard her breathing settle into a natural rhythm and I knew it was safe to go to her.

She was laying on her side facing the window and the blankets were pooled around her waist. I saw the rise and fall of her chest in the tight tank top, the creamy swell of her breasts barely visible and felt my stomach muscles clench in response. I sat on the edge of the bed and probed her subconscious with my mind.

She was immediately receptive to me and I slipped into her dreams, closed my eyes and seduced her with my mind. She opened her arms and I gathered her to me, inhaling her scent like a drug. I smoothed my hand down over her back and over the rounded curve of her hips and she moaned as she pressed herself against me. I took her face in my hands and kissed her very gently and before I could stop her, she crushed her lips against mine, her body demanding more from me than I had given before. It felt so sensual, so real and so incredibly right.

I felt my fangs start to grow and I opened my eyes and watched Sierra writhing on the bed. She stopped as she sensed my withdrawal from her mind and whispered into the dark,

"Come back to me, I know you are there,"

She was still fast asleep and I slipped back into her dream to talk to her as I removed my clothes and got into bed beside her.

"I'm right here, my love," I whispered as she opened her mind wholly to me and bared her soul. There was nothing about this woman that I did not already adore, every single thing about her called to me. She was the other half of my tarnished soul.

A smile lit her face in our dream and my chest constricted painfully at how beautiful she was. I could feel her emotions and she radiated happiness. When I opened my eyes briefly to look at her physical form again, I saw the same smile mirrored there.

It was time.

"Do you know what I am Sierra?" I asked her softly as I slipped back into her consciousness and she stared at me with those beautiful violet eyes for an age before she spoke.

"I think so," she murmured, but I felt no fear coming from her, only curiosity and arousal.

She had the ability buried deep inside her to sense what I was and as I caressed her body lightly with my hands, she watched my face and put her finger to my lips. I opened them slightly and she ran her fingers over my teeth, pricking the tip on my sharpened fang. She withdrew her hand and looked at the spot of blood before she spread it on my lip for me to taste. My tongue tasted her and it sent a jolt of electricity through my body, I could feel the feral animal inside me crying to be set free and I needed to wake her.

"Sierra," I whispered, "Come to me, my love. Open your eyes and come to me,"

I eased out of our dream and I gathered her body to mine as I waited for her to come fully awake. The feeling of her semi-naked body in my arms was almost too much to take, my body was on fire from wanting her and she moaned at my withdrawal as I tried to soothe her. Her heavenly scent was my undoing. I felt the change in her and I lay perfectly still as she awakened.

Her eyes flew open and searched my face and I felt her emotions change, not to fear but to relief when she reached out and touched me to see if I was real. Her hand smoothed down my body and over my chest but I held her gaze, she had to take the lead here, I didn't want to frighten her. I could still sense her arousal and I was struggling to keep control as her hands touched my body, exploring me from my lips to my rigid torso. Finally, I could stand it no more and thought I might burst with longing and I flipped her onto her back and covered her body with mine.

Her excitement was palpable and she pulled my head towards her to kiss me. I pulled the tank top over her head and felt the fabric of her lace panties rip before I tossed them on the floor. Before I went any further, I had to show her what I really was and I leaned back, drawing back my lips so that she could see my fangs fully extended.

She stared at me but I felt no fear from her, only

curiosity and desire

"Are you going to bite me," she asked calmly and I had to suppress a smile.

"Only if you want me to, my love,"

"Will it hurt much," she wrinkled her brow

"No," I smiled "Just the opposite,"

She nodded and I leaned over and took the rosy tip of her breast in my mouth, everything about her was designed by the goddess for me to desire, her looks, her taste, her smell. I reached down and touched her between the legs and she bucked up to meet my fingers caressing her. I traced my tongue down her body until I reached her core and tasted her, my tongue teasing and pleasing her at the same time. She tasted like heaven.

She was bucking and writhing beneath me and urging me to take her. After weeks of making love in our dreams, I knew we would come quickly together. I positioned myself between her thighs before I captured her mouth in mine and thrust inside her.

She bit down on my lip when I entered her and felt resistance, I realized with a shock that I was her first. I had known she was fairly innocent but hadn't realized how much so and I stilled inside her. I was so afraid I had hurt her but she showed no signs of distress and I felt her body start to tighten around me as I rocked into her and I smoothed my tongue over the soft spot just below her ear so that she would not feel my bite.

When she started to cry out, I sunk my fangs into her neck and tasted her life force and she screamed, not with pain but with the heightened ecstasy of our blood bond and moments later as I pulled from her, I cried out her name. I felt our combined emotions crashing through me as our mental link snapped permanently into place. I hadn't been fully prepared for the sensations running through me as we bonded and felt utterly euphoric. Sierra was like a powerful drug and I was her addict.

I smoothed my tongue over her neck to seal my bite and watched as the marks already started to heal on her smooth skin. She was truly mine now forever and I had never felt anything like the connection we just shared, despite my many, many years.

I wrapped my arms around her and she snuggled

closer.

"What does this mean," she whispered,

I touched her face and closed my eyes and showed her in her mind, what I was, who I was and what we could be together.

She gasped as I broke the connection and turned her lovely violet eyes to look at me and asked,

"Are you going to change me too, to be like you?"

"Yes," I answered simply "But not yet,"

"I don't even know your name," she gasped,

"Yes, you do Sierra, close your eyes and concentrate,

She nodded her understanding as I opened my mind to her, she had seen all that I am and understood that our destinies were entwined. I was shocked and inordinately pleased by her lack of fear and her ability to accept me and what I was and it made my frozen heart swell.

"Luca," she smiled and I knew mother was right, Sierra was destined to be the other half of me, my soul bonded, my mate.

I leaned over her and claimed her lips again and when she wrapped her legs around me I knew my life would never be the same again.

CHAPTER SEVEN

Sierra

The fruity smell of her favorite shampoo did nothing to remove Luca's scent from her, not that she wanted it too, she only needed to close her eyes and she could smell him, taste him. She knew what he was, a vampire, some part of her had known since he started visiting her in her dreams, weeks ago. She pushed the thought aside and allowed her desire for him to flourish. He didn't frighten her, but she had seen it in their connection, that not all of his kind would be as welcoming to a human.

He was concerned that he had hurt her the first time but she brushed it aside, she had never felt like this before, she didn't know sex would be this amazing. She knew he had bitten her but she hadn't felt it, she only felt his lips on her neck and her orgasm had suddenly intensified until she thought she couldn't bear the sweet pleasure a minute longer, he was amazing.

His voice, like the rest of him, exuded sex appeal, sometimes when he whispered to her, she detected a very slight difference in his accent but more than that, sometimes he spoke like he was from another time and place.

She wrapped herself in a towel and dried her hair, leaving it to fall loosely around her shoulders. She dressed in a brown suede skirt, soft cream silk top and brown leather boots, applying a little makeup. She rarely wore any but she wanted to look her best today.

She had called Brynna and asked her to work her shift at the diner today and her friend had happily agreed. Like her, she needed the extra money.

Luca was coming to collect her to take her to 'The House' for dinner tonight to meet his parents and brothers. He had explained to her and she saw it in their connection when he projected that she was now Luca's mate. In his world, they were linked mind, body and soul, a stronger link than marriage in her world. Luca called it a soul bond but the link would not be complete, at least in the eyes of the council, until they had undergone a claiming ceremony where he would claim her as his mate for all eternity.

She felt a little bubble of nervous laughter escape her lips at the absurdity of her situation and had to pinch herself to make sure she wasn't dreaming. She was linking herself to a man, no, a vampire, who she had only just met and slept with, for all eternity! She had felt something tangible when their minds linked but she didn't truly understand it all just yet. She only knew she had been waiting for Luca her entire life.

She was nervously pulling at invisible pieces of lint on her blouse when he pulled up in front of her house and she ran to meet him. He grinned at her enthusiastic greeting and swung her up in his arms.

He wore dark dress pants and a white open neck shirt and she thought he looked like a GQ model. She breathed in his scent as he helped her into the car and her head was swimming with emotions and questions.

"Are you making me feel these things for you Luca?" she asked him bluntly,

"No," he took her hand, "We can use the power of

suggestion but not even my mother can control free will," he smiled indulgently at her questions as he pulled the sleek car onto the road. He didn't add that witches practicing black magic had been known to do just that, he didn't want to overload her with information just yet, or frighten her.

"I have so much to learn," she sighed and he raised her hand to his lips,

"I am happy to teach you, my love. Close your eyes and take a deep breath, Sierra. Relax and open your mind to me, imagine sharing your thoughts,"

She felt something nudge at the periphery of her mind and she asked him if he was doing that, not out loud but inside her head and she giggled when he answered her the same way.

"Concentrate," he said sternly, "This is important. This time I want you to try and stop me from entering your mind, block the connection between us, try to keep me from hearing your thoughts,"

She looked at him with her large violet eyes and he melted and added softly,

"Please Sierra, it's important that you are able to block others from feeling your emotions or even from reading your thoughts.

She closed her eyes again and when she felt the nudge, she imagined a wall being built brick by brick in the inner recesses of her mind until she could no longer feel his presence there.

He looked at her incredulously,

"You did that on your first try,"

She couldn't stop the grin that spread across her face and the pleasure she felt from his praise and she shrugged,

"It wasn't difficult,"

"Try again and this time see how quickly you can do it, ready?"

She nodded and he mentally nudged her mind but got nothing in return, he glanced at her and she looked smugly back.

"It took me many years to learn how to do that," he said and she felt herself blush and a warm feeling flooded through her at his approval.

He brushed his fingers over her pink cheeks and she felt the heat pool in her stomach and her heart began to beat faster,

"I should turn the car around and take you back to bed," he murmured and laughed as her cheeks turned even pinker and he felt her arousal coursing through her. She slammed her mind closed to him and he shook his head, chuckling,

"Sierra you are a natural,"

"Will I have to constantly be on my guard for people probing into my head," she asked,

"No, I'm the only one who has that open connection because we are bonded but you can still shut me out and I will respect that. You may feel people trying to get in but unless you open your mind to them, they won't be able to hear your thoughts. Only a very powerful and ancient vampire would be able to force it and no one of our House would do that without permission, my father would flay them if they tried."

She was trying to take it all in when they stopped at the side of the road and pulled over into a grassy area just off the road.

She looked at him quizzically and he took her hands in his,

"Tell me what you can see Sierra," she looked around and shrugged, wondering what he meant. "I have blocked our connection, now watch as I open it and look again when you see it through my eyes,"

She felt the energy flow between them once more and looked around in amazement. Where there had only been trees before and the gated entry to an overgrown field, suddenly she saw a long, sweeping, tar-covered driveway, lined with trees and protected by a tall red brick wall and heavy imposing gates.

She was shaking her head in wonder at this new world she was now a part of. Luca drove on for several minutes, passing houses, farm buildings and curious people on either side of the road, until they came to a stop in front of an impressive two-story, sprawling mansion with a circular driveway and a beautiful, color changing fountain in front.

Sierra gasped out loud as she took in the sight in front

of her,

"Holy crap Luca, are you royalty or something," she looked terrified,

"My mother is five centuries old and my father twice that age, it's easy to amass a fortune when you live so long," he brushed it off and came round to help her out of the car. He took both of her hands in his, leaning down to kiss her again before dragging himself away.

"Let's go meet my family".

CHAPTER EIGHT

Luca

I watched Sierras face with pride as she mastered mind blocking easier than a child with a lollipop. She knew instinctively what to do and I guessed she was unconsciously unlocking and mastering the elven part of her DNA. She still hadn't figured out for herself that she wasn't fully human. Together, we would help her realize her full potential but for now, I had to help calm her nerves before she met my family.

She was nervous and who could blame her, she was about to enter a house full of vampires a day after finding out we existed.

I could feel her hand shake a little as I clutched it in mine and the door opened in front of us. A servant stood aside to let us pass and I saw Sierra roll her eyes at the pomp and ceremony of our House. I nudged her mind and she opened automatically to me.

"These people are very proud of the jobs they do for our family, they would not be pleased to think you mock them," I chided her and she had the grace to look a little contrite.

I took her through to the drawing room and we found everyone there waiting for us. I felt her hand tighten in mine and I squeezed it back.

"Mother, Father, this is Sierra Adam," I introduced her to my parents and saw her eyes widen with surprise and heard in her thoughts, she liked my mother's fairly modern taste in decor.

My mother came across the room and gave her a brief hug and welcomed her warmly into our family.

"Your home is lovely and I am so happy to meet all of you," Sierra said and as my father took her hand in his and I could also see the approval in his eyes. My father didn't have the ability to read minds, despite his age, but he could sense if someone was being untruthful.

My brother Ettore shook hands with her a little stiffly and I saw her look closely at Finn and Ronan as they each hugged her, they looked alike but were not identical twins. Aeric was the last to greet her but my little brother wrapped his arms around her and kissed her on the cheek, much to my surprise.

She kept her mind open to me but she blurted out in typical Sierra fashion

"Wow, you are all so good looking," which caused a ripple of laughter from my brothers.

"Come sit with me Sierra, so that I may come to know you better," my mother urged and I watched as she dragged my mate off to the sofa to chat. I felt Sierra relax as my mother fussed over her.

My father poured her a glass of wine and then turned to me and I nodded and joined him at the bar. I sipped on my red wine,

"How are things going so far Luca," my father asked quietly and I couldn't stop the smile that split my face as I answered him.

"Father, she is amazing. She has taken all of this in her stride and it must feel absolutely surreal to her,"

My father chuckled as he looked at Ettore and I saw him scowl back before he turned his back on us.

"I think your brother is deliberately resisting this process but your mother assures me the girl, Greer, is his intended," Ettore walked away out of earshot and I whispered to my father.

"Don't be so sure father, he has been watching her," I smiled, which brought another smile from him as Sierra nudged into my mind and I removed all thoughts of Greer.

"Your family are amazing Luca,"

My father escorted her into dinner and my mother took my arm. I could see he was charming her and she was holding her own. She glanced at me from time to time but she seemed to be quite happy and not at all out of her depth. I could tell my family approved of her and in time they would come to love her, and although it would have made no difference to me in the end, I was pleased they saw in her what I did, Sierra would be a good fit here.

We took a walk in the garden after dinner and I pulled her into my arms as soon as we were away from the house and kissed her until we were both breathless. She melted into me and ran her fingers over the tip of my fangs until she drew blood and encouraged me to lick it off. Immediately I felt my muscles tighten at her taste and she chuckled as she played with me. I opened my thoughts and projected them to her and she gasped as the images of us together floated into her mind and I felt her emotions surge through her. She was aroused and happy.

"Luca, take me home," she whispered as she tightened her hold on me. I grinned and took her hand as we walked back to the house. At the door, I turned to her and surprised myself.

"Move in here with me," I asked her and at her surprised look, "There is no point in waiting my love, we are bonded now. Move in with me, join my House and let me hold you in my arms every night."

She barely hesitated a moment before she nodded and I lifted her in my arms and raced upstairs to my rooms with her. I had always intended for this to happen but thought it weeks from now, however, I was pleased that like me, she saw no point in waiting.

She was a little dizzy from the speed at which I can

move and I held her against me until she gained her equilibrium. Eventually, she turned away from me to explore what would become her new living quarters. We were standing in the bedroom and I saw her eyes focus on the bed in the middle of the room before she shielded her thoughts and turned to explore the rest.

"The fact that you are shielding your thoughts from me lets me know exactly what you are thinking," I laughed and she rolled her eyes,

"Not exactly," she said with a smile as she opened the door to my sitting room and then the bathroom and another empty room on the other side of the sitting room.

"What's this room for," she asked and then quickly realized "A nursery," she said as she dropped her shield and I saw in her mind she was carrying an infant in her arms. The image jolted me for a moment. I wanted so much to bury myself in her and plant my seed right now. The feeling was primal but I wanted it more than anything else in this world, apart from possessing Sierra herself.

She was unaware of the times she asked a question

and then answered it herself before I had a chance to speak, she really had incredible insight and her gifts would only get stronger the longer she spent in my world.

I took her hand and led her to the sofa.

"Sierra, close your eyes. Now, can you look inside yourself, deep inside and feel the other part of you that's been hidden, for a very long time, another part of you that you know is there, you can feel it when you close your mind to me or when you let me into your dreams. Humans can't usually do that, but you can, what is the other part of your self Sierra?"

I watched as she concentrated on delving deep into herself and thought I might have expected too much from her as I saw her wrestling with something, her face screwed up in concentration. I sat in silence for a long time as she burrowed deeper and deeper into her subconscious. I thought again that maybe I was asking too much of her, too soon. I reached to tell her we would try again another day when suddenly her eyes flew open and she looked at me in awe,

"Luca, I'm part elf, my Grandfather was an elf," she said incredulously as her hands flew to her ears and I chuckled at her funny antics. "I didn't think elves were real and I always hated my ears so much. Now I know why they are a little pointed," she said and then saw the funny side of that statement, sitting here across from a full-blooded vampire and burst out laughing.

"Luca, there was something else there too, but I couldn't quite grasp it," she said a puzzled look on her beautiful face. "It kept evading me but it had something to do with my Grandma."

I certainly didn't see that one coming and had no clue what she was referring to. I would have to talk to my mother to find out what else Sierra sensed inside herself.

CHAPTER NINE

Sierra

'Luca's mother is beautiful!' She thought, a little in awe. She had glossy black hair tied up in a loose chignon and very expressive dark brown eyes. She was very warm and friendly and Sierra instantly relaxed around her. She thought his father very handsome too and looks a little older than his mate, but not by much. He too has dark hair but his eyes are green and she sensed kindness and generosity in him but could sense a darker side too. She got the same feeling from Luca on occasions but in him, it truly excited her.

Luca and his brothers all looked like they stepped off the cover of GQ magazine but she was indifferent to them all in that way, apart from Luca. She wondered if all vampires were good looking and Luca smiled as he nodded an affirmative.

"Everything about us is enhanced when we are

changed, the good the bad and sometimes, the ugly," he explained in his thoughts.

Aeric teased her a little and she liked him immensely, he had a young, carefree personality that made her smile. The twins were friendly too, Finn she knew would be a charming rogue and Ronan had an easy, quiet persona that drew you to him, but Ettore was a little distant and she sensed he was conflicted by her presence here.

The food was excellent and sitting here eating with them she thought they seemed like a perfectly normal, nice family. They teased each other and argued just like anyone else. The servants hovering around seemed a little strange to her but she hadn't rubbed shoulders with many wealthy people and she guessed she had a lot to learn. She knew instinctively they were mainly vampires, one was better looking than the next but she sensed that the pretty girl serving them dinner was something else entirely. She would ask Luca later.

She was surprised by Luca's invitation to move in with him now but she guessed he had a point, why wait if they were irrevocably bound to each other. It just meant she needed to do something with her Grandma's house. The truth was she hated being away from Luca. She couldn't explain it but it was painful if he was gone for too long, in person or in her dreams.

She said her goodbyes to his family and knew she would see them again very soon. Luca didn't want her to wait to move in with them, there was an urgency in his request and she instinctively felt that he was keeping something from her, she aimed to find out what it was.

She had liked the rooms he lived in, they were fairly private and she guessed with the size of the house that his brothers all had suites like this too. It was like a large, airy apartment within the house.

She loved the furniture and color scheme in here and knew it was exactly what she would have chosen for herself. She loved the mixture of old, like the original crown molding and picture rails and the new, like the flat screen tv in a cabinet at the bottom of the bed. The opulent king-sized bed and matching dark wood furniture was a perfect foil for the pale pastel colors on the walls and covering the bed. Windows covered the length of one wall and there were double doors leading onto a veranda.

The living room was shades of gray and blue with soft comfortable sofas, an open fireplace and a small dining table tucked into the corner of the room, she guessed Luca sometimes preferred his own company for dinner.

The bathroom was bigger than her bedroom at home and had a huge walk-in shower, double vanities and double closets on either side of it. The empty room on the other side of the living room was the one that intrigued her most. She had guessed correctly that it would eventually be a nursery and she had already seen into Luca's mind that he wanted her to bear his children. It was part of his father's plan to continue the house but she could see in Luca's thoughts it was much more than that, his genuine desire to have a family with her. She felt like she should be insulted somehow, but she wasn't, she wanted this as much as he did and it would have to be before she was changed, to become a vampire like him.

She would move in here with Luca and his family but she also had a job and her Grandmas house to take care of and she still wanted to finish her degree, it would only take a couple of months at the most. She projected this to Luca who nodded his assent.

"Find a tenant for the house if you don't want to sell it, but Sierra you must know as my mate you do not need to work, in fact, it would be better if you didn't. The fewer people that wonder about where you now live or about my family the better,"

She felt a stir of annoyance in her belly and he took her hand,

"Sierra, when you become like me people will eventually start to wonder why you do not age and it takes a little time to reign in your strength and speed to go unnoticed in the human world. You will also have to learn to control your thirst for blood." She sighed but stayed silent. She didn't like it very much but knew he had a valid point.

She had an urge to talk to Greer about all of this but she guessed that Luca would not approve. She had only known her for a short time but they had become quite close, very quickly, another strange thing in her very strange life.

She felt Luca nudge her and she opened her mind, she loved that he always asked permission. He saw her thoughts about Greer and smiled as he projected. 'You will be able to confide in Greer soon my love,' but not just yet. She didn't ask why, she trusted Luca completely.

He made her tea in her small kitchen as she changed into her pajamas and he had stripped off down to his shorts. He looked right at home wandering around her house half naked and she could barely keep her eyes off of him. She opened her laptop and placed an ad in the local paper looking for a tenant to rent her Grandmas house, she still wasn't sure about selling but this would give her a little time to think about the future.

She sipped her tea as she typed and when she had finished, she checked her email to find that a good many of her Grandma's jewelry pieces had also sold and she printed labels and stuck them on padded envelopes to ship them out. She needed to go to the bank tomorrow with the cash she had found and pay the rest of her bills and she would be solvent for the first time in a long time. It was a good feeling.

She yawned and Luca set aside her laptop and sent her upstairs to bed while he locked up the little house. She was a little sleepy but wanted more than anything to lie with Luca in his arms and feel his lips on hers. Her heart missed a beat as she shielded from him and smiled to herself. She discarded her pajamas before she climbed into bed completely naked.

CHAPTER TEN

Luca

I was glad Sierra went off to bed without a fight because I wanted to check on something without her knowledge. I pulled on my pants and slipped out of the back door quietly while she was upstairs. I closed the link between us and quickly picked up my brother's scent, following it to the garden of a house a few down from Sierra's. I sneaked up on him while he was preoccupied watching Greer through the window of her kitchen.

He snarled at me when I touched his shoulder and I knew he was annoyed and embarrassed that I had caught him here watching her.

"You must have known I would pick up your scent Ettore," I teased him as he made to jump down from the branch we were perched on.

"No, stay," I told him as he continued to avoid looking me in the eyes, "I am going back to Sierra," I grinned.

Just as I made to jump down, he grabbed my arm. He continued to stare at her for the longest moment.

"You seem happy with Sierra," he said dragging his eyes from Greer to meet mine at last,

"I am brother, she is truly my mate. I am complete with her and you will be too, just trust yourself and your feelings," I patted his shoulder, "Have you visited her in her dreams," I asked and his pale blue eyes wavered as he turned back to watch her.

"No, not yet, but I know she senses me whenever I am around her," he said at last,

"Go to her Ettore" I urged him and his face relaxed a little as he smiled,

"I think I will."

I slipped quietly back into the house and went upstairs; I had only been gone a few minutes. I could tell by her breathing she was not yet asleep and my stomach clenched as the heat engulfed me, good, I was not done with her yet tonight.

I discarded my clothes and felt her naked skin as I

pulled her against me and loved that she had anticipated me. I smoothed my hand over her belly and she turned to lie on her back. I pulled back the sheets and put my lips where my hands had been seconds before and she smiled as I nudged her mind and asked if she wanted me.

"You know I do Luca, always," she said aloud and run her own hand over her flat stomach and I imagined her swollen and round with my child inside her and I had such a feeling of euphoria I had to close my eyes for a moment. She nudged my mind and I saw her thoughts were in sync with mine.

I felt my fangs growing already, I had barely touched her and she giggled as my erotic thoughts flowed between us.

She sat up and swung her leg over me, sitting on my hips and I knew she could feel my erection beneath her as she ground her hips into me. I growled as I gathered her to me and took her breast in my mouth, I bit down a little and heard her gasp but could sense that she was enjoying it immensely. I teased her other nipple between my thumb and finger and she was already coming apart in my hands.

I opened my eyes again and she was looking at me through her thick sweeping lashes, her eyes misted over and it took all of my willpower to hold back when she raised her hips and slid herself on to me. I let her set the pace as she moved on me, but I could sense that she was already almost there and licked the skin at the side of her breast to numb her when she grabbed my hair and pulled my head back to the other side and looked at my fully extended fangs and said breathlessly

"No Luca, I want to feel it when you feed from me," she smoothed her finger over my fang and pierced her finger and smearing the blood onto my lips.

I didn't want to hurt her but could see in her mind she wanted to feel the pain as well as the pleasure so when she closed her eyes and started to keen, I leaned in and bit her. She cried out, her muscles tightening around me before the sensations swamped her and she writhed on top of me and I instinctively began to suck.

I came quickly and almost violently and have never felt anything so pleasurable, so intense in my many, many years. For as long as I pulled, she was still drunk on the sensation but I was forced to stop because she was still human and I didn't want to take too much blood. I sealed the bite and she whimpered as she came down from the high and she started to cry, great big wracking sobs.

I felt like someone had cut out my cold stone heart as I held her to my chest but she nudged into my mind and I could see the emotions had just overwhelmed her, she wasn't crying because she was sad, she was crying because she was so happy.

"Did it hurt too much when I bit you, Sierra," I asked her and she shook her head no,

"Just a little pinch but I loved it, I always want to feel you when you bite me, Luca, you don't need to hold back."

I could feel myself stirring again at her words but I lifted her from me and she put a pillow under her bottom as she lay down again, resting her head on my chest and at my puzzled look she laughed,

"I read somewhere that doing this can increase the chances of pregnancy and I want to carry your baby more than I can say."

I very much doubted the science behind it, but I loved that she wanted it to happen so soon. I fell asleep with a smile on my face.

CHAPTER ELEVEN

Sierra

The smell of grilled bacon was tantalizing but she lay contentedly in bed thinking about last night. She thought at one point she was going to pass out, the feelings were so intense as they made love. She had been a little afraid of his naked bite but a part of her, a primitive part, wanted so much to feel his fangs pierce her flesh and knew afterward she would never want to be numb again. The flash of pain was countered by the seemingly never-ending, exquisite pleasure that had swept her body. She wondered if it was this good for Luca.

"Yes Sierra, it is," he said as he came into the room, smiling, with a breakfast tray for her. Sometimes she forgot about the mental link and unconsciously shared everything with him.

She patted the bed and he sat with her as she polished off bacon, eggs and toast and a mug of coffee. He didn't eat anything but he had coffee and he watched her silently as her eyes wandered over his lean sculpted muscles. He wore nothing but boxers and she leaned over and ran her fingers over his chest and smirked as he sucked in a breath.

"We have many things to do today my love," he said standing up out of her reach but she saw the effect she had on him clearly and couldn't help the chuckle that escaped her lips.

He grinned almost painfully and she felt a shiver run through her as she watched his blue eyes begin to glow brighter again and she knew he was as affected as she was.

"I would like you to move in with me as soon as possible, I can help you pack and be out of here today," he said changing her train of thought and she nudged him to see why he was so impatient but he remained shielded to her.

"What's the rush," she asked and a look of annoyance crossed his face quickly before he turned his back to her, pulling on a shirt and jeans. When he turned back his face was a mask of composure and she crossed her arms stubbornly and waited. He was shielded from her and she raised hers in childish retaliation. He sighed and came towards her taking her hands in his.

"Now that we have bonded Sierra and it's probably known who you are, there are those who would not want to see our union completed by the claiming ceremony.

Every house has enemies but if my father's plan to see us settled with our mates and children comes wholly to fruition, we would be stronger than ever and there are some who do not want to see that happen. I do not know to what lengths they would go but I won't take that chance with you. You will be fully protected anywhere on our estate and my mother has surrounded it with many layers of security but until you are changed and can protect yourself, you cannot ever be alone again."

Sierra felt her anger rise that he had kept such a vital piece of information from her and stood up, shaking her hands loose from his as she stomped into the bathroom and slammed the door in his face. She heard him growl on the other side but he made no attempt to follow her.

She turned on the shower and stood underneath, letting the hot water beat on her until her anger subsided a little. He should have told her the whole story from the very beginning, it infuriated her that he hadn't trusted her with this information.

She felt a frisson of fear run down her spine, someone, probably more than one wanted to kill her and Luca forgot to mention the fact when he fucking entered her dreams, wooed her into bed and tied her to him for eternity. She knew that she would eventually change to be like him, sometime after she had children but now she had no choice. Whoever wanted her out of the picture would probably try and kill her while she was still human.

She dried herself and went into the bedroom, sensing Luca was downstairs. There were jeans and a white cotton top on the bed as well as a lacy white bra and matching underwear and she felt her ire growing stronger again as she yanked open the wardrobe door and found all of her clothes gone, the drawers on her dresser were empty too. She dressed quickly and marched downstairs just as he was coming in through the front door.

"I packed your clothes, Sierra, they are in the car," he said as he ran upstairs and a few seconds later he was back with her toilet bag and placed it on top of the box standing by the door. In it she saw the parcels she had to mail out and the remaining jewelry that had yet to sell as he picked up the box and took it out to the car.

Running her hands through her hair in frustration she went into the office and opened the safe to get the money to pay her bills and retrieved the receipts from the drawer and stuffing them all in her purse, resigned to doing what he wanted for now.

He came back in again from the car and pulled her into his arms, holding her closely,

"I do not mean to frighten you, I just want to keep you safe," he said softly and despite herself, felt her anger melt away at his touch.

CHAPTER TWELVE

Luca

I didn't handle that very well; I knew how stubborn and independent Sierra could be and I should have warned her at the very beginning of the dangers of our bonding. However, even if she had rejected me completely, she would still have been in mortal danger, just in the fact that she was my soulbond, our enemies would rather see her dead than risk even a slight chance that she would change her mind and complete the bond with me. It is why mother kept her identity from all of us until the last minute, even although she has known who my intended was for many months.

I smiled as I thought back to how angry I had been that my parents were trying to choose a mate for me. I had mirrored Ettore's horror as such a thing and had refused to consider it at all until curiosity had won over and I followed her home one night. I hadn't been prepared for the sucker punch that hit me in the gut when she turned my way and I saw how perfectly beautiful she was.

Her eyes were the color of violets and her thick blonde hair tumbled around her small heart-shaped face. When she parted her full lips to smile and wave at her neighbor, my body had reacted immediately and I was hooked. My every waking minute since then revolved around Sierra and what I had to do to make her mine. It was more than falling in love, it was a meeting of minds and souls and her very existence and mine were inexplicably linked.

I opened my mind to her as she sat beside me in the car, I knew she was still a little peeved if not outright angry. I let all of this flow to her to help her understand that since the moment my mother knew of her existence she was probably in danger, I just hadn't yet realized it.

After a few moments, she reached out her hand and squeezed mine although she kept her eyes on the road in front of her. I thought I saw a hint of tears in her eyes but she clearly didn't want me to see them so I kept quiet. It pierced my cold, dead heart that I was the cause of her pain.

I took her hand and pulled her up the front steps to our home and handed the keys to one of the servants to bring in Sierra's belongings and put them in our rooms. I swept her up into my arms and carried her across the doorway as she squealed and struggled for me to put her back on her feet.

"I know it's traditional for humans to carry their brides over the threshold of their new home," I grinned as I swung her around the hallway.

"I'm not a bride," she said smiling and I nudged into her mind, not yet, but very soon my love.

I was much happier now that I had her under my protection and could breathe a little easier, I vowed to do everything in my power to make her happy here.

Breathlessly she giggled and struggled out of my arms and we made our way to the sun-room where I knew my parents would be this early in the day. I was surprised to see my brothers there as well and I knew by the atmosphere in the room that something was amiss. I sensed my father's anger and my mother agitation. My brothers were all silent as they waited impatiently for us.

My father stood abruptly as we came in and mother took Sierra's hand and drew her forward to sit beside her on the loveseat. Mother chanted an incantation and I knew she was shielding the room from prying ears.

"I heard disturbing news a few minutes ago but waited until you were all here to explain," he began but he was looking at me as he spoke and I had such a feeling of foreboding from him I instinctively crossed to place my hand on Sierra's shoulder. "It seems our enemies are in greater numbers and are moving faster than we anticipated. Your mates are all in grave danger and they must be brought here immediately for their safety. Do what you have to do to achieve that, today."

My father indicated Sierra on the sofa with my mother.

"Sierra is safe here with us, Luca, go with Ettore and I will go with Aeric. Kai and Toran will go with Finn and

Ronan, he indicated the two men who had just entered the room. There is no time to lose," He strode for the door, brushing a kiss on my mother's head as he passed her by.

I knelt before Sierra, seeing the questions in her eyes and kissed her hands. She nodded to me and whispered,

"Go, we can talk later," before I hurried out after Ettore who was already running full speed for the front door.

My car was still parked out front so we jumped into it, my father and brothers already gone. As we sped along the road, I cloaked us from human eyes with a little glamour to aid our journey.

Ettore and I could probably run faster to Greer's house but we needed to bring her and her belongings back with us. I wished I had more time with Sierra to explain about Greer and just as I had the thought she filled my mind and I realized she could still link even from this distance, her gifts were increasing in strength but her thoughts were confused so I pushed my barrier into place vowing to talk to her as soon as I got back and hopefully before she saw the other women.

I slowed right down as we approached her house and I sensed she was home alone. I nodded to Ettore and parked the car around the back before I slipped into the house as he knocked on the front door.

As she was distracted with Ettore I entered her bedroom and emptied her closet, drawers and personal belongings from her bathroom and packed them into three suitcases I found in the guest room. I was super quick, while Ettore kept her downstairs and I had them all moved out and packed in the car as Ettore came out through the back door a short time later with Greer in his arms. I grimaced, that part hadn't gone to plan and he had rendered her unconscious. He placed her in the back seat and climbed in beside her as I quickly reversed the car and sped towards home.

Even in her sleep I could feel the anger emanating from her and I chuckled at my brother's stony face, she was not going to be happy when she awoke.

In the rearview mirror, I saw Ettore gather her to him and lay her head on his shoulder, stroking her long red hair as if soothing her and I thought this was a different man from the one who had stood nose to nose with our father, refusing even to consider this match. I too could relate, in only a few weeks of watching her, Sierra had bewitched me, mind, body and soul.

Ettore carried Greer to the sitting room and laid her gently on the chaise as she slept, we waited for the others to arrive. I was hoping my mother was filling in some of the gaps for Sierra while we were gone so that she would not be too appalled when she discovered her friend was among the women we brought here. I sensed them at the other end of the house in my mother's suites and I guessed she was keeping her away from us for the moment.

Ronan and Finn arrived back soon afterward with their mates, but we kept them separate for now too until we had a chance to explain. Ronan took Darci to the library, she too was asleep and Finn was in the sunroom with his mate, who was wide awake and giving him hell, he had tried to force her to sleep but it appeared she was resistant to his powers as well as his charms and he was using brute strength at the moment to try to keep her calm.

We had to wait a while longer for our father who had sensed another presence in Aeric's intended's home and had got there just in time to prevent a tragedy. Two vampires had been laying in wait for her when she got home from work and she had fought back snarling and clawing like the undiscovered wolf shifter that she was until one of them had thrown her across the room and knocked her unconscious.

Sorcha Stillwater was Aeric's mate, but he had never met her until today. He sat beside her on the sofa in the den and wiped the blood from her skin to see the extent of the damage. She was healing quickly, thanks to the lycan blood that flowed in her veins but Aeric cut into his palm and let his blood drip onto the worst cut on her stomach and watched as it healed almost instantly, the skin knitting together and leaving an angry pink scar. She visibly relaxed then and he stood to pace the room. I could see the conflict in him for a woman he had only just met and I understood it only too well.

Thankfully my father and Aeric had easily

overpowered and slain the two unknown vampires, turning their bodies to ash. Father said they had refused to talk. He was right, things were escalating far too quickly for comfort.

I looked around me and everyone was contained so I went in search of Sierra, I had a lot of explaining to do.

CHAPTER THIRTEEN

Sierra

Violette was doing her best to distract Sierra as she showed her around her rooms and she was genuinely interested in some of the beautiful pieces Violette had collected over the years. She had a stunning collection of Fabergé eggs and Hendrik had a passion for collecting snuff boxes, but after a while, the distraction was no longer working and she couldn't stand it any longer. Violette sensed the fear in her and put a hand on her arm.

"They will all be back soon, he is safe Sierra," she soothed her, "But I would ask that you don't judge him too harshly when he does return."

Sierra wrinkled her brow in confusion and reached out to Luca with her mind. The connection was stronger and more powerful each time she did it but he was blocking her. She sighed in frustration and Violette smiled.

"You remind me so much of me when I was young you know" her laughter tinkled as she spoke but before Sierra could reply, she felt Luca's presence in the house and ran for the door.

"He is here, I can sense him," she announced.

She ran through the hallways and saw him coming out of the library, closing the door behind him. She launched herself at him throwing her arms around him and wrapping her legs around his waist as he held her tightly against him.

"Luca, I was so worried about you," she sighed as she breathed in his distinctive scent.

He ran quickly upstairs, still holding her until they got to their rooms. She kept her eyes closed for a minute until the dizziness stopped. And felt herself being lowered onto the bed.

When she opened her eyes and looked at him, he brushed her face with his hand.

"Everyone is safe my love, but we really need your help,"

She waited for him to continue

"These women will be frightened and confused, we need your help explaining to them what is going on. Unlike you they know, or at least sense what we are, but my brothers do not have the advantage of getting to know them before all of this happened,"

Sierra nodded and held out her hand to him as she climbed off the bed,

"Let's go then," she said and hurried toward the door before he had a chance to warn her about Greer.

They walked back downstairs hand in hand and they went to the sitting room first where Ettore was standing guard outside the door.

"She is awakening now," he said aghast as he looked from one to the other, "She is going to hate me for all eternity,"

Sierra raised her eyebrows at him and opened the door and stopped dead at the sight of her friend Greer laying on the chaise, her long red hair spread out behind her. She threw me a dirty look before finding her feet and she ran to her, kneeling on the floor she took her friend's hand in hers just as she opened her eyes.

"Sierra," she questioned as she helped her sit upright and she looked beyond her to Luca behind and back to Sierra,

"I know you are confused Greer but I will try my best to explain to you what's going on," she said softly to her friend and Sierra felt a nudge on the edge of her mind and opened up, gasping when she realized it was Greer probing into her mind and not Luca. They sat in silence for a few minutes and Luca watched in wonder as his mate and her friend communicated, he knew Sierra was growing day by day but this blew his mind. Greer he knew was half-elf and sensed she was something else too so she wasn't a surprise but his face split into a grin as he watched Sierra.

Greer's head snapped up and she turned her clear green eyes on Luca and said,

"Where is he?"

Ettore came into view and Sierra heard her friend's intake of breath as she watched the tall, handsome man approach.

"It's you," she accused as Ettore kneeled in front of

her and Sierra knew instinctively Greer had seen him in her dreams too.

Greer seemed calm if somewhat annoyed and Sierra and Luca felt they were intruding on a private moment left quietly closing the door behind them.

"How did you connect with her," Luca asked her shaking his head,

"I felt her nudge me and I opened up, it was quicker to show her than to try and explain," she smiled and he trapped her against the wall, an arm on either side and kissed her.

"You are amazing, do you know that," he said as she wrapped her arms around him. She was soon wishing they were alone and when she felt his fangs lengthen, she scraped her tongue along the sharp point drawing blood, knowing he would not resist the chance to taste her. As he sucked, she felt him harden against her and pushed away from him.

"Down boy," she grinned and turned from him and sprinted towards the library where she sensed she was needed next.

She only got a few steps before Luca pounced and had her pinned to the floor, caging her with his arms. His eyes glowed brighter blue than she had ever seen them and she swallowed as she recognized the predatory look on his face, his fangs fully extended, his face inches from hers and his breathing labored. She knew he was struggling to control himself.

"You should never, ever, run from a vampire Sierra," he chastised "When we chase it's either to hunt or to mate.......or both," she felt her arousal erupt in her belly and heard him chuckle as he ran his teeth slowly along the length of her neck without breaking the skin. She opened her mind and he invaded it with erotic visions of them and she whimpered, wanting so much to race upstairs with him to the privacy of their suite and strip the clothes from his body.

He sighed and stood up, pulling her with him,

"We will revisit this later," he said regretfully, regaining control, as he pulled her towards the library door but she could feel the waves of desire emanating from him.

Darci Breedlove was awake when they went in and she was sitting beside Ronan calmly as she absorbed everything he had just shared with her. They hadn't met in person before but he had obviously been in her dreams before and Sierra could see her intense attraction for Ronan already in her eyes.

She was an adorably cute platinum blonde with huge blue eyes peeking out under her bangs and Ronan was hanging on her every word with adoration.

She shook hands with Darci and felt the spark as they touched and Sierra could feel the magical pulses surrounding her. She gently nudged the other girl's mind and Darci grinned as she gave her access, were all of these women gifted in some way? They shared their stories in just a few moments and knowing the calm, gentle blonde was by far the least of their worries, they went looking for Aeric.

Aeric's intended, Luca told her in as they made their way to the den, was called Sorcha Stillwater and she was part lycan.

"As in wolf?" she swung round to look at him and he

nodded. She noticed his teeth were still part way extended and she chuckled and walked on and heard him growl behind her.

"You will make it up to me later my love," he said quietly as he patted her bottom and her stomach tightened in anticipation.

He mentally explained about the two vampires who had tried to kill her earlier today before Aeric and his father had got to her. Sierra felt a shiver run through her. This was indeed a dangerous new world she had entered.

Sorcha was still asleep and Sierra felt nauseous as she took in the blood and the torn clothes, she mentally asked Aeric about her clothing and he streaked from the room and returned with a clean t-shirt. Sierra eased the bloodied, torn shirt from her body and replaced it with the clean one.

Sorcha was extremely pretty with thick, milk chocolate hair and thick dark lashes that were still resting on her cheeks as she slept.

"Her wounds have healed but she is resisting coming back to us," Aeric said and Sierra placed her hand on the girl's forehead. She instantly felt her intense, emotional pain and instinctively started to draw it from her, surprising herself. She was unaware of her surroundings as her palms heated up and she felt the tension start to seep from Sorcha's body. She felt her pain and sorrow as she drew from her. She saw the girl's eyes start to flutter and took her hand, holding it tightly in hers as she regained consciousness. Their thoughts were flooding between them and when she opened her eyes Sierra saw that they were a beautiful warm, golden brown with orange spikes rising from the irises.

"Thank you," she whispered to Sierra and reached the other hand out for Aeric.

He looked a little surprised by her gesture, then puzzled, but Sierra patted his shoulder as she stood up to leave,

"She saw my thoughts Aeric, the rest is up to you."

She turned to the doorway and Lucas's mother stood there with a strange expression on her face and took her arm as she passed her, asking an unspoken question.

Sierra shrugged but she was fatigued and knew that

whatever just happened had drained her strength.

"I don't know how I knew to do that, I just did, something is different when I am in this house," she said quietly to Violette's questioning look as Luca followed her out into the hallway once more.

He held her around the waist, marveling at his mate's astonishing gifts as they went to find Finn. Afterward, she was going to bed for a much-needed rest.

They heard the commotion before they entered the room and Sierra looked to Luca who shook his head and grinned,

"I think Finn may have met his match,"

Sierra stared open-mouthed at the broken ornaments and shattered panes of glass as she walked into the sunroom and Finn was trying desperately to dodge whatever missiles the pint-sized female was launching at him.

"I hate you, Finn, I should have known you were trouble when I first laid eyes on you and if you think I am going to be your mate, you have another think coming," she screamed as she yanked the lamp free of the socket and aimed it at his head.

Sierra turned to the furious girl with the coal dark hair and flashing amber eyes and screamed as she threw out her arms,

"Brynna!"

She looked up and forgetting Finn for a moment, launched herself at Sierra, laughing and crying at the same time as Sierra tried to fathom what the hell Brynna was doing here. They had only worked together a short time but she liked the dainty spitfire very much.

Finn looked enormously relieved at the respite from her violent outbursts and went to his brother who couldn't help grinning.

"You got what you deserved this time brother, you're made for each other," Finn sighed but his bright green eyes kept straying back to the fiery beauty now wrapped around Sierra.

"How much has Finn explained" Sierra began

"Enough," Brynna glowered at him but Sierra picked up her attraction too.

"Well I don't know if you're part elf, Lycan, witch or

hell even vampire," Sierra said throwing her hands up in the air as she set her down but let's try this as she nudged Brynna's mind and the other girl chuckled as she opened to her.

After a few moments of connection, while Sierra sent the other woman her thoughts, Brynna seemed to calm down just a little but she looked at Sierra and laughed,

"I'm half fae, my father is from the faerie realm, my mother was human," and Sierra looked at Luca, the exhaustion finally catching up with her.

"I need to lie down, we can catch up later," she said, kissing Brynna on the cheek and shaking her head as she walked out the door to go to bed.

"Wait, I think you may need this girl," Brynna called and took Sierra's hand, chanting an incantation and Sierra felt a rush of energy enter her body just as Bryna let her hand go.

"Thank you," she smiled as Luca picked her up into his arms and she felt like she had been teleported back to their rooms.

CHAPTER FOURTEEN

Luca

I had been burning for her for what seemed like hours now and my fangs hadn't completely receded and they wouldn't, not until I had drawn blood. I couldn't wait to get her alone and get my hands on her naked body. Until Brynna had given her a boost of energy I thought I would have to wait until she slept and rejuvenated but now...

I kicked the bedroom door shut with my foot and barely gave her time to get her bearings, still holding her with her legs wrapped around my waist I captured her mouth roughly and she bit down on me drawing my blood and savoring the taste. I knew the few drops wouldn't be enough to do anything to her, only give her a little strength, but she moaned as she tasted me and it sent me into a frenzy.

I held her against the wall with my body as my hands pulled the top over her head and ripped her jeans down the middle until they lay like rags on the floor. Sierra pulled my shirt front and the buttons popped off and I knew she wanted this as much as I did. Her chest heaved in the white lace bra and I unhooked it with a snap until her breasts were free, the taut nipples rubbing on my chest.

I mentally nudged her to ask if she was sure this is what she wanted, until now our lovemaking had always been fairly gentle and she screamed yes in my head as she reached for my jeans, freeing my erection and I ripped her panties from her as I pressed against her entrance, she opened up to me and I pushed hard inside her as she whimpered and I thrust into her again and again as she came apart in my hands and moved her hair to the side, exposing her neck. I could smell the blood pumping through her veins and I sunk my fangs into the soft delicate skin and she screamed my name over and over while I pulled from her.

As I came, the emotions I had been holding back, slammed into me and I clung to her as if my very life depended on it. For the first time in over two hundred years, I felt the taste of salty tears on my face. I gently licked her neck to seal the bite and held her until her heart rate slowly returned to normal.

We were mated and bonded by our souls but there was more, I loved her, I loved her more than I had ever loved anything or anyone in my entire existence.

I kept the knowledge to myself for now as I thought she had enough to deal with but as we lay naked in the bed and she slept soundly, curled up in my arms I wanted to shout it from the rooftops. I never knew I could be this happy.

Sex was just sex to our kind, a pleasurable way to pass the time and we indulged in it frequently, but once mated it would be extremely rare for one of us to stray from our bonded.

Others no longer appealed to us like they did before and sex is ultimately very much sweeter when there is a bond. I knew my father had never taken another lover since he met my mother which would be incomprehensible to a human but it's who we are.

I felt Sierra stirring and when she turned in my arms

to face me, she opened her mind and I saw her thoughts clearly.

"I want to make love to you and drink from you again too Sierra but it's too soon my love," She hooked her legs around me and gazed at me with those beautiful eyes and I gave in and folded her warm body to mine. It was tender and sweet and when we came together, I kept my fangs sheathed this time, with much difficulty, but it was still beautiful nonetheless, it always would be with her.

I chased her out of bed and into the shower and I asked Alya, one of the young elven servants to bring her something to eat.

She sat on top of the bed wrapped in a towel, her wet hair falling loosely down her back and sipped as we talked about the other women that had arrived today. I was surprised she wasn't angry with me about Greer and Brynna but she seemed to understand that it was for everyone's safety that she didn't know about them. Darci and Sorcha, she didn't already know but she would soon enough.

I chuckled again as I thought about my brother and

112

the handful he was taking on in Brynna and at her quizzical look I opened my thoughts and Sierra grinned.

"Poor Finn," she smiled and then burst into another fit of giggles.

Changing the subject, I told her my parents were hosting a formal dinner for them tonight so that everyone could get together and get to know each other a little better. My mother loved to entertain and we promised her this once a week to keep her happy.

"I don't have any formal clothes," she stated, shrugging her shoulders and I walked to the bank of closets and opened the furthest door revealing an array of new dresses and matching shoes beneath that the servants must have brought up earlier in the day.

"Courtesy of my mother," I said dryly, but Sierra just laughed, not in the least bothered by the fact that my mother had picked out several outfits for her to wear.

"I'm sure I will find something among these," she stated matter of factly and hopped off the bed to look at the beautiful dresses hanging there.

Violette had got her to a tee, Sierra thought as she fingered the fabrics and pulled out a lovely strapless, empire waisted, chiffon in a gorgeous amethyst that Luca thought matched her eyes. There were matching sandals underneath and she brought them over and laid them on the bed.

"I will wear this tonight,"

I left her to dry her hair in front of the dressing table and went to shower, smelling her scent as the water washed over my body.

I had come back into the bedroom dressed in pants and a shirt when I heard Alya, who I guessed mother had asked to look after Sierra, enter our suite. She talked non stop while she worked her magic on Sierra's hair, braiding and pinning it in place. I stifled a grin at the camaraderie Sierra had already struck up with the girl, she had that effect on everyone. She was questioning her on her elven heritage and Alya was happily filling in the blanks. Sierra was shocked to learn that Alya was already over forty years old, but she explained that was very young for an elf.

She explained that both of her parents worked on the estate, her mother was a healer and her father the head of estate security and her sister Alys would be attending to one of the other young ladies.

Sierra said she felt like something out of a Jane Austen novel but a stern look from me had her bite her tongue. As I explained to her before, these girls coveted their jobs and were proud of them. There were many elves living among the humans but they had to hide what they were for fear of persecution. Here on the House of Van Buren estate, they could just be themselves.

Alya helped her into her dress and she sighed as she felt the fabric drape over her body. She slipped on the shoes and looked at herself in the mirror as I came up behind her and fastened a beautiful diamond and amethyst necklace around her neck, I handed her the matching earrings and she fastened them before turning around to look at herself again in the mirror. She fingered the jewels and I saw in our connection she was wondering how I guessed which dress she would choose to wear.

"They're beautiful Luca, thank you," she said aloud,

She looked amazing and I know she saw the approval in my eyes but for now, I kept to myself that I had jewels of every color and gemstone for her to wear. I didn't want to overwhelm her. I remembered something and sped out of the room saying I would be right back.

A few minutes later I came back into the bedroom with three snow-white rose buds that she took from me and tucked into the braid of her hair. She touched them gently before a smile stretched across her face and she reached up to kiss me.

I tied my bow tie and donned my jacket and I heard her catch her breath. She was good for my ego and as she opened her mind to me and I caught a glimpse of the images she was projecting I slid my arms around her waist and leaned down to kiss her

"Later, I promise," I said and she shivered.

CHAPTER FIFTEEN

Sierra

Luca's parents were in the drawing room when they went downstairs and Violette came towards her, hands outstretched.

"Sierra, you look wonderful, that color is perfect for you,"

Sierra thanked her and repeated the compliment. Violette was stunning in silver chiffon, her glossy black hair falling down her back like a sheet and the smooth perfection of her face.

Hendrik brought her a glass of champagne and they sat down to wait on the rest of the family.

"Did Brynna manage to wreck any more of the house," Luca asked grinning and his mother rolled her eyes as she answered,

"It's Finn's own fault," she replied her lips twitching into a smile "He should have been more honest with the girl from the start. I knew his reputation could end up being a problem,"

Ettore ushered Greer into the room and Sierra thought her friend looked amazing. She wore a dark green, one-shouldered silk that hugged her slim figure and her hair had been twisted into a low chignon that suited her elegant stature.

Sierra rose to greet her, enveloping her in a hug and when Ettore held out his hand to shake Sierras she pulled him into a hug too that surprised him and everyone else, but he didn't pull away. Luca brought them champagne and Violette smiled and took her hand.

"Come, Greer, sit beside me," she urged and Greer followed her to the sofa,

Ronan and Aeric came in next with their intended mates, Sorcha was dressed in cream colored silk with her thick hair curled and tumbling loose and Darci wore navy blue satin. They both looked a little shell-shocked and immediately made for Sierra. She hugged them both sympathetically as Aeric and Ronan brought glasses of champagne.

Violette spoke to them both kindly but didn't make a move to touch them just yet. She seemed to know how far to push with each girl and for now they were looking to Sierra for comfort.

They made small talk among themselves and she saw Violette look at her husband wondering where Finn and Brynna were when the door opened and he came in looking more than a little pissed and exasperated and Brynna breezed in past him, her dark hair hung softly down her back and surrounding her beautiful face, her amber eyes flashed as she greeted everyone. She was wearing a fit and flare royal blue organza that seemed to float around her tiny frame, she looked gorgeous.

Finn handed her a glass of champagne which she snatched from him and swallowed in one go and then swapped her empty glass for his. She came across the room to hug Sierra, ignoring Finn as he followed her. He shrugged and got himself another glass and Sierra heard Luca ask if things were any better.

"She will kill me before this is over," he said as his eyes followed her and Luca caught her eye and smiled.

Brynna was not making it easy for him.

She asked him mentally if Brynna and Finn were sharing his suites and he replied no, the girls were staying in the suites and his brothers were in the guest rooms until such time as they were invited to share.

"So what you're saying is no-one is getting any action but us," and he grinned at her raising his glass and she shivered as his eyes held hers

"We shall make up for them tonight too," and she felt her cheeks flush,

She turned from him to catch Violette watching her and she blushed even more but she came towards her and took her hands.

"I am amazed by your abilities so far Sierra, and I cannot read you or Luca's thoughts but the pink tinge in your cheeks gives me the general idea," she teased her and Sierra blushed even more.

She noticed the other girls watching her with Violette and Greer looked a little envious, but it was only because Violette had known her a little longer. Greer had been alone most of her life and she craved a family more than anyone. Violette would become a good mother in law to all of us, she thought.

Luca escorted her into dinner and held out her chair. Luca was on one side of her with Hendrik on her other at the top of the large, dark wood table. The servants brought course after course of beautifully presented dishes and the food was melt in the mouth delicious. Luca touched her thigh, mentally asking her if she was okay and she replied the same way with a smile. She felt at home, even with the pomp and ceremony of the plush dining room and the dozens of servants.

The others were starting to relax a little now and with the exception of Finn were building relationships with their intended. Brynna was cordial and charming to everyone else but pointedly ignored him. This seemed like any other large, often dysfunctional family and Sierra relaxed and enjoyed the rest of the meal.

They retired to the drawing room and some of the furniture had been pushed back to allow room for dancing. Hendrik went to the built-in stereo to put some music on. Sierra loved to dance and when the first bars of one of her favorite songs began to play Luca swept her into his arms and they danced as he held her close.

She danced with each of his brothers and his father too and she couldn't remember when she had enjoyed a more lovely evening. She drank a little more champagne that gave her a nice warm buzz and she noticed Ettore and Greer were dancing cheek to cheek too, she could feel attraction for him coming from her friend in waves and she hoped that meant that she was accepting her fate to be Ettore's mate.

Just as the night was winding down, Brynna was deliberately flirting with Ronan, who was doing nothing to encourage her but enjoyed watching his twin squirm nonetheless. Finn finally snapped.

"Screw this," he shouted as he thrust his drink into Luca's hand,

She heard the growl coming from him as he stormed across the room picked Brynna up like she weighed nothing and slung her over his shoulder as he marched out of the room, the door banging behind him. They could hear Brynna demanding to be let down as their voices faded. Sierra focussed on Finns departing form and could feel a little anger but mainly frustration coming from him and she chuckled,

"Brynna may get more than she bargained for tonight," she whispered and Luca started to laugh too.

No-one else seemed at all concerned as they all said their goodnights and went to bed.

She walked slowly upstairs with him, holding onto his arm and stopped when they noticed Ettore standing in front of Greers room with her. He lifted her hand and kissed it before he strode away and she went inside and closed the door. Sierra knew the attraction was there in spades and really hoped it would work out. They looked perfect together.

She kicked off her shoes, hung up her dress and unpinned her hair, shaking it loose before she walked to Luca's outstretched arms in her lacy underwear. He picked her up and threw her down on the bed with a growl, covering her with his body and she let out a sigh and wrapped her arms around his neck as she welcomed him.

CHAPTER SIXTEEN

Luca

Tonight was a bit of an eye-opener for me as I watched Sierra mingle with the other women. They looked to her for some kind of leadership and she was unwittingly providing it to them. They were drawn to her and as my mate would help me rule the House of Van Buren in the unlikely event anything should anything ever happen to my father. She would effectively become what my mother had always been to him.

Sierra was unaware of the effect she had on others and tomorrow I was curious to see how she would fare as she and the other women would begin their training. They needed to learn to defend themselves in case of attack. I could protect her, but until she was changed, I wanted her to be as prepared as was humanly possible, and in a very short space of time.

I lay in the dark just holding her as she slept and

marveled at the joy she brought to my existence. When we had made love again, I felt like an adolescent boy as I struggled to control myself with her. She had opened her mind fully to me and the images she projected drove me crazy with lust, she knew the effect she had on my body and I knew she enjoyed the power it gave her over me. I smiled as I buried my face in her hair, drinking in her scent and slept like an infant until dawn.

This morning Sierra was beyond excited that she was to have lessons in self-defence and my father's head of security, Daeron and two of his best warriors Kai and Toran would assess the women's potential and help train them to the best of their abilities.

After Alya had laid out appropriate clothing for her to wear she had practically bounced downstairs to eat the breakfast I insisted she eat. We left the women alone as my brothers and I caught up with our father to forge ahead with further plans to enhance the security of the estate to protect those within its walls.

The others greeted Sierra warmly as she sat down to eat breakfast with them and I knew they would have many questions for her. I closed the door behind me and I left them to it.

Ettore was scowling at something father said as I joined them in the study and I realized the change in him. He was desperately worried about Greer's safety which brought a smile to my lips as I realized my brother was no longer resisting the pull to her as he had been for weeks but was falling for the girl and anxious as to how he could best protect her now. I could also feel his shame that he had once deemed a human mate to be beneath him as I could see the pedestal that he had placed Greer upon.

We discussed plans to strengthen the perimeter security with the humans in mind and although no one had dared breach it before, our spies tell us there are those out there who would do so now. We had a duty to protect not only them but everyone who made their home here with us on the estate.

When we had finished our meeting I wandered out to the training yard to watch Sierra go through her paces with the others but kept myself hidden from sight. I knew my brothers were almost certainly doing the same thing as I could sense them and picked out their scents among the trees.

I looked around and spotted Finn, high on a branch, watching Brynna sparring with Kai, a vampire with extraordinary fighting abilities. She was pretty good and light on her feet, but no match for the larger man. I could feel the magic surrounding her and thought she may be better placed learning more about her gifts from my mother or one of the fae that lived on the estate.

Daeron called Greer forward as Brynna threw herself on the ground beside the others to rest. Greer's sparring was also fairly good but she was quick. They sparred a few rounds and he swiftly moved on to something else. When he handed her the bow I saw something change in her stance as she lined up and placed the arrow on the bow and drew back before releasing the dart high into the air. I watched with awe as she hit the target first time and as she practiced she hit the mark time after time. With the long braid hanging down her back and her awesome bow skills, Greer looked every inch the elf she was born to be.

Sorcha sat quietly watching the training and when she

was called up she fought well, was quick-minded and light on her feet and unsurprisingly, very fast. Daeron called Marcus forward and he sparred with her for a while, deliberately goading her until she fell flat on her face and jumped up to face him, her eyes glowing orange and a feral snarl echoed around the yard. She stilled when she realized it was coming from her and Marcus grinned, took her by the arm and walked off into the woods with her. Aeric bounded after them to watch. She was half Lycan and I got the sense that Marcus, a full-blooded wolf shifter, suspected she was unconsciously suppressing her natural abilities.

I knew Darci was going to be working mostly with my mother but she still needed the physical training to get her as fit as possible. She was half witch and my mother had vast knowledge and many gifts of her own, being a witch herself before becoming a vampire.

Sierra was the only one left and as Daeron called her forward he asked her to touch each of the weapons in turn and see if anything called to her. She lifted the bow and fired off a few arrows and she had a decent touch but not in Greer's league.

She picked up a sword and swung it around and put it back down again and then I felt, rather than saw something stir in her as she walked to the table and picked up a belt full of combat knives. She fastened it around her waist and walked forward to the wooden board set up as a target. I saw her take a deep breath as she removed three of the knives and watched her gauge the weight as she balanced it in her fingertips. Daeron called out to her

"Sierra, close your eyes for a minute and imagine that there are intruders, vampires who are unbelievable fast and their sole aim is to leave no-one here alive, you have three seconds GO!

In a flash I saw the three knives sail through the air and land smack in the middle of the target as she dropped to the ground and rolled to the side, another three knives ready to throw. I jumped down from my perch and stared at her in amazement, at this moment in time she looked like a warrior with her thick blonde braid, swinging behind her and her lean, lithe figure in combat clothing, her hand poised on the knife belt. The expression on her face was fierce and I felt something stir within me, I had never been prouder of her.

Daeron put his hand on her shoulder and chuckled

"I think young Sierra, we have found your weapon of choice.

CHAPTER SEVENTEEN

Sierra

Sierra felt a tingling inside her that grew to the tips of her fingers when she held the knives in her hand and she knew instinctively how to handle them. When she had held the heavy sword she knew she could probably never wield it properly to be of any use to anyone and after watching Greer with the bow, well, that was a nonstarter, but when she balanced the knife on her fingertips it felt like an extension of her and she knew she wanted to pursue this as her choice of defensive weapon.

Daeron had given her a belt of knives to keep and urged her to practice as often as she could to hone her skills. She smiled with pleasure as she fingered the cold hard steel of the quality knives. They had sparred some more with each other and their trainers before calling it a day, the fitter she was in case of combat, the better.

She relished the steaming hot shower after her heavy

workout and was pleased to see Luca sitting on the bed waiting for her when she came out. He wore snug fitting jeans and a white t-shirt that showed off the bronzed muscles in his arms. She groaned at the distraction and quickly dressed as he watched her with a smirk on his handsome face. She slammed her shield into place which amused him even further.

He had promised to take her to town today to mail off the last of the jewelry she had sold and to pay the last of her bills. She had a potential renter for the house and wanted to meet them too and she also needed to go into the diner and tell Sal and her workmates she wouldn't be coming back to work, planning to tell them she was moving across country to get married but that she would be around from time to time which would cover her in the event she was ever spotted around town.

They completed their errands fairly quickly and she really liked the young couple that wanted to rent the house and directed them to the attorney's office to sign the lease. She would have him deal with it from now on.

She pushed open the door of the diner and Sal came

around from the back when he saw her, concern written on his weathered face. She apologized for not telling him sooner but gave the cover story and accepted everyone's congratulations. He told them that Brynna called and said she had gone back to California to be closer to family and wouldn't be coming back either, except for visits. Sierra acted surprised but felt guilty at the same time, Sal had always been very good to her.

They sat at a table tucked in the corner and a brand-new waitress brought them coffee with a smile. Sierra ordered a cheeseburger and fries and Luca shrugged and ordered the same but she sensed that something was bothering him as his eyes darted around the diner and he seemed to be on edge.

She opened up to him and mentally asked the question, rather than risk being overheard and he replied that he could smell the residual scent of a vampire here, possibly two and that he didn't recognize them. His eyes were wary and constantly darted around as they ate.

He paid the bill and she was happy to be going back behind the heavy security of the estate. Just as they were leaving Sal called out to her that two men had been in asking for her and Brynna yesterday but he had told them he didn't know where they went. She knew immediately that they weren't men but vampires, the ones who's scent Luca had picked up on.

She shivered as Luca helped her into the car and sped along the road to get back home as quickly as possible. She was relieved when they finally pulled off the road and came to a stop in front of the house. Luca's face was stern and she knew he was thinking what could have happened to her, and to Brynna, if they hadn't acted when they did

They hurried along to the study to speak to his parents who took the news very grimly that they already knew where to look for Sierra and brynna, plus the attack on Sorcha, which probably meant they knew about all of them, Darci and Greer too.

"Until further notice, the girls don't leave here unless absolutely necessary and even then only with at least two guards, preferably Daeron, Toran or Kai," Hendrik barked out as Luca's mother came into the room. They brought her up to speed and she paced back and forth before she said,

"Whoever is behind this has access to powerful magic to see through the layers I created to hide the girl's identities, but I also suspect that we may have a spy in our midst."

Sierra shivered again,

"Luca says you can sense the truth in people," she said looking at Hendrik, a question in the statement,

"I can indeed but we do not want to alert them that we know. I could line everyone up and ask them questions and probably scare them in the process but I don't want to forewarn," his face was grim and they fell silent as they contemplated their next move.

Violette put her hand on Sierra's arm,

"You will be safe here," she smiled her reassurance but Sierra could feel anger in her gut that someone wanted to harm her friends and her new family.

She left them discussing how best to fortify security and went looking for the other women, finding Brynna and Darci in the sunroom. They were practicing some simple spells and she joined them, enjoying the company of the other women to take her mind off what she had learned. Darci felt drawn to potions and herbs and was going to take some lessons from Violette and Brynna already had a little experience with telekinesis.

"Here let me show you," she offered Sierra,

She watched as her friend closed her eyes and began reciting a spell, she opened them again and concentrated and reached her hand out for the glass on the table and watched in amazement as is slowly slid across the surface toward her.

"Now your turn," she told Sierra and had her practice the enchantment several times before she talked her through the rest.

Sierra closed her eyes, took a deep breath and tried to move the glass, but nothing happened,

"Open your mind fully and concentrate," Brynna said,

She tried again and this time as she chanted, she slowly opened her eyes and imagined the glass sliding across the surface toward her and was startled when it flew across the table to land squarely in her hand,

"Wow," said Brynna and Darci shook her head in amazement,

Sierra sat back on the chair and wondered not for the first time how she was able to command her mind to do these wonderful things.

She took a deep breath and told Brynna and Darci about Luca sensing that vampires had been in the diner and sal saying they had been asking after them and as they talked Greer and Sorcha came to join them.

"I don't know about you but I am not going to wait around for them to come and get me," Brynna said angrily, her eyes flashing, "I think we should have a plan, be prepared for them coming for us and not just rely on the vamps to keep us safe."

The others nodded their agreement and looked to Sierra who felt the same anger stir in her gut and she stood up, pacing the sunroom,

"We have already proved we have a little skill; we are not helpless females waiting on our mates to protect us, we need to be able to do that for ourselves. I suggest as well as the training we have with Daeron every morning that we need to work on our other gifts as well. I feel as though I have untapped ability but I may need help in reaching it and I know just the person to help."

Sierra's face was a mask of single-minded determination and the vampire smiled as he watched and listened from high up in the trees. She was the one he had to kill first, preferably before she was claimed but he would kill her anyway, before or after. He felt a stirring in his gut as he imagined all the ways he would like to do it.

CHAPTER EIGHTEEN

Luca

The women wanted to explore the estate and Kai and Toran were dispatched by me to watch them from a distance. My father had already absolved them both of any wrongdoing, he trusted them with our lives and so did I.

I could hear her at a distance now and occasionally she opened up her mind to let me know where she was and I chuckled when I saw her astride a horse getting a lesson from Feredir, a young elf who looked after the stables. I could feel her pleasure emanating through the connection and felt my chest constrict. I knew that she had ridden before but I suspected it had been some time ago. I would ride out with her tomorrow, give her a chance to hone her skills further, I wanted to do everything in my power to make her happy.

I spoke briefly with my father and brothers and father

had news this morning that our enemies were planning something big and the word was that it would most likely be at my claiming ceremony. We hadn't yet decided when that was going to be but I wanted to avoid it at all costs. I felt sick at the thought of Sierra being in danger.

"Luca, my son. Avoiding the ceremony will just make them look for another way. At least this way we can be in control of the situation and preempt what they are likely to do," my father placed his hand on my arm.

I was angry but I knew he was right but I needed to talk to Sierra, she and the others had a right to know they were going to be 'bait', and they also had a right to refuse.

I didn't see her again until dinner as we had much to plan and my father was making a list of those we could trust implicitly. After we had eaten, casually tonight, we gathered in the library where father had the plans of the estate laid out on the table. My brothers Finn and Ronan, with Daeron, had been charged with making sure every corner of it was secure.

There would be vampires coming from other Houses

across the country, some we trusted and some we did not and Ettore and Aeric with our mother and her abilities would comb them for any sense of threat.

I took Sierra aside and told her my father's plan before we told the others as it was her claiming ceremony as much as mine. She looked grave but nodded her assent and I again marveled at my mate's ability to accept what was, with courage and without complaint.

My brothers would not be claiming their mates at this time. It was a solemn, serious matter that would officially make her a Van Buren and allow her the protection of our laws, so Sierra was most likely going to be their prime target as to harm her after the ceremony would be a grave crime indeed. It meant however that having the chance, they would likely try and harm the other women too. None of them, or us were safe.

We gathered everyone together and explained what we knew already and I was proud that the women took the threat so seriously.

"Be careful about guarding your thoughts against others and if you need to speak openly with each other,

141

come in here to the library. Violette has soundproofed it from eavesdroppers with a charm," my father added talking to the women, "To charm the entire house in this way permanently would require too much of her magic and would weaken her but this room is safe."

We dispersed to head off to bed and Sierra hung back with the other women and mentally asked me for some time alone with them. I kissed her lightly on the lips, inhaling her sweet scent and took my brothers into the game room for a nightcap, giving the women some privacy. I knew they had a lot to process and were bonding in a different way, a little like sisters.

Ettore demanded to know what they needed privacy for and I suppressed a smile, he was a little over protective and I had a feeling Greer would not necessarily appreciate it. Finn was still battling with Brynna but they seemed to have called a tentative truce for the moment, I guessed as they both had bigger fish to fry right now.

I left my brothers after a quick drink and went upstairs to shower. Sierra was still downstairs with her friends and I opened a connection to her but she was shielding and I had to wonder what they were up to. I dried off and went to bed, drifting off to sleep as I waited for her to join me in our bed.

I felt her presence before I saw her and she leaned over me and brushed her lips over mine. I was instantly awake and pulled her to me for a kiss. Her hair tickled my face and she chuckled as I squeezed her butt cheeks in my hands. She pulled back from me and I watched, getting more aroused by the second as she slowly stripped off her clothes, making a show of each item as she tossed it on the floor. I let loose a low growl and I could see the excitement in her eyes and she unsnapped her bra and turned on her heel walking into the bathroom and tossing her golden hair over her shoulder.

She opened up to me and I saw vivid images of us both in the shower, her legs wrapped around my waist, my face buried in her hair and I sprang out of bed and got to the bathroom door before her.

She chuckled as she turned on the spray and slipped her panties off and came towards me and pressed her naked body against mine, reaching up on her toes to kiss

143

me. My excitement was obvious and I lifted her up and backed into the spray with her as she shrieked with laughter. I loved the feel of her soft skin beneath my hands as I caressed her body and tasted her sweet lips. She wrapped herself around me tightly and I wanted to claim her now but I also wanted to savor her.

I lifted her until I could take her breast into my mouth and sucked hard on its rosy tip as she gasped and tightened her hold on me, fisting her hands into my hair. I could feel her pulsing against me but I resisted and reached my hand between her legs, circling and caressing her with my fingers and she moaned with pleasure at my touch. She was urging me inside her but I waited as long as I could, continuing to kiss and caress her, until she threw her head back in abandon and I bit into the tender flesh at the side of her breast and she lost control, crying my name as I quickly thrust inside her and pulled on her at the same time.

We rocked together under the warm water, she was still convulsing as I came quickly and I felt such a rush of ecstasy that it was almost painful and my legs began to shake. As we came back down to earth together I shut off the water and she watched as I gently sealed the bite on her breast and it instantly began to heal.

"What will it be like when I bite you after I am changed," she asked me and my gut clenched at the thought of how intense it would be, I knew I couldn't wait to find out.

CHAPTER NINETEEN

Sierra

Sierra snuggled in Luca's arms after they made love and marveled again at how quickly he had weaved his way into her heart, mind and soul. She was afraid, not of the direct threat against them but rather that she could lose this bond, this affinity, she had built with him in such a short time if either of them were killed.

They had talked late into the night and had finally agreed that their claiming ceremony would take place here on the estate, in two weeks time. She had a lot of work to do before then. Luca wanted to wait a little longer but she felt if it was too long their enemies would find another way to get to her and her friends before then and he reluctantly agreed with her.

She had talked with the other women last night too, closing off her mind to Luca as they talked and they felt the same way as her. They were not going to rely solely on the men protecting them, they had to take an active part in their own safety. Granted they had yet to tap into all of their supernatural abilities but they weren't completely powerless either.

Brynna and Darci had agreed to help teach her what they already knew and had newly discovered and the five of them were going to physically train with Daeron for three hours each morning and several more hours honing their minds. She could already feel her muscles toning, her mind getting stronger and she could move small things at will now, she wanted to be in the best shape of her life before the ceremony.

Darci was going to work on some spells with her too. She had managed to create a shield around the five of them as they sat in the grass outside the stables this morning, to prevent their voices being heard by the sharp ears of the vampires and elves around them. It would come in useful to keep their plans to themselves and she was trying to teach Sierra how to do it too. Their philosophy was quite simple, the more they could hone their skills to protect themselves the better for everyone.

Sierra still felt another presence inside her, she searched in vain but she was sure there was something more, just out of her reach and she wanted to ask Violette for her help.

She knocked on her door just after lunch, Luca was somewhere on the estate with his father and brothers and she and the other women had trained with Daeron and Kai this morning. She felt invigorated after the workout, they were really putting them through their paces and the cool shower afterward gave her skin a healthy glow.

There was no answer so she wandered out to the garden and found her on her knees tending her roses. She stood when Sierra approached, dusting off her hands to hug her. Luca's mother looked very human today in her jeans and t-shirt and a sun hat pulled over her long, dark hair. She smiled as they walked and she guided her in through the open doors of her sitting room, removing her hat and gardening gloves. She closed them firmly behind her, waving her hands and she heard the lock click into place and felt the hum of magic as she sealed the room from eavesdropping intruders.

She already knew that it would drain his mother too much to permanently soundproof and protect the entire mansion so the library was the best choice for a permanent charm and she could seal others at will for short periods of time without using up too much of her energy.

"I wondered when you would come," she smiled at her again and poured them both a glass of iced tea from a tray on the table. She gestured for her to sit and she perched on the edge of the sofa, waiting for her to speak.

Sierra took a sip and placed her glass on a coaster on the glass topped table and then asked her future mother in law to help her unravel what it was that she felt was still trapped inside her. Violette studied her for a while as she played with glass in her hand.

"This is something you have to do on your own Sierra," she said at last "There is an untapped, powerful resource inside you, I can sense it, have felt it since the moment I first saw you, but it has been shielded from others by strong magic and I believe it was done to protect you, a gesture of love maybe. Only you can unravel it my dear but I do feel that it is near the surface and you only need to reach out and embrace it,"

Sierra sighed suspecting that it would have been too easy for Violette to just tell her outright. She nodded and thanked her knowing deep down it was down to her to figure it out but she didn't think it had hurt to ask.

"However, something I *can* help you with," she smiled broadly as she pulled Sierra towards a large dressing room accessed through her bedroom. Sierra noticed the same mix of old and modern furniture that graced the rest of the mansion but her attention was drawn to a hanging rail with at least a couple of dozen dresses in a variety of colors and styles.

"You need a dress for your claiming ceremony!" she exclaimed as she urged her forward to look at the beautiful fabrics in front of her. "We traditionally don't wear white as you do at weddings in the human world, but this is essentially just like a wedding and you can wear whatever you choose Sierra, it's your day."

She fingered the fabrics and mentally told her that she already had a closet full of beautiful, unworn gowns

Violette already bought her,

"Nonsense, she brushed the idea away. They are certainly lovely gowns Sierra, for a formal dinner or for attending someone else's claiming ceremony but not your own. You need something special. You are my son's mate and he is the heir to our House."

Despite herself, Sierra looked through them and reached for a snow-white Chantilly lace, goddess style gown. With tiny lace cap sleeves, an illusion neckline and a plunging, open back. It was utterly gorgeous and she needed very little persuasion as Violette urged her to try it on. It was fairly lightweight apart from the beautiful elaborate train and fit her body like a second skin, until a few inches above the knee where it flared out dramatically. She turned to look at the back and she fell in love with it.

"I could wear white roses in my hair and really look like a bride," she said almost to herself

"It's your day, you can have whatever you like," Violette said indulgently.

She reached for a panel in the wall and pressed a

button and a few minutes later a petite, vibrant woman bounced into the room. She didn't look elven or vampire and Sierra knew she must be fae.

She gave off the same energy signal as Brynna. Her crystal green eyes sparkled and her bright red hair was short and spiky. Sierra could almost see the faint aura surrounding her.

"Sierra, this is Isadora, she is wonderful with a needle and thread."

Isadora went into a cupboard in the dressing room and brought out a sewing basket. She started to pin the dress at the front to lift it from the floor and Sierra had an idea.

"Would it be possible to have the lower part of the dress and train detachable from just above the knees," she asked and the dainty faerie smiled,

"Of course dearie, anything is possible, you just leave it to me.

She removed the beautiful gown and gave it to Isadora and got dressed again before bidding them both goodbye and went in search of her mate.

She chuckled as she thought about the gorgeous dress

and the claiming ceremony that was fast turning into a wedding, she hoped Luca would be fine with all of it, his mother was determined to make a celebration of their ceremony one way or another.

She opened her mind and reached out and she could feel him smiling as she made her way to the stables to find him. She had been practicing shielding parts of her mind and leaving others open. Violette said it could be a useful tool for a human as other vampires would not realize she was shielding at all. She had only had limited success with it so far.

Their horses were saddled and ready to go and she knew Luca was a better horseman than she was but she managed to keep up as he raced ahead and she felt the wind whip her hair out of its loose braid and stream behind her as they sped along. She felt exhilarated but was slightly out of breath and her thighs hurt from holding on so long when they finally slowed down. Luca jumped from the saddle and came around to lift her down and set the horses loose to drink from the pond.

She threw herself on the grass and groaned. Her fair

skin was tinged pink and her hair was mussed and windswept.

"My thighs hurt," she laughed and he kneeled down and started to rub her legs starting at the inner thighs and working his way down. She sighed as his strong hands massaged her and she felt the heat start to pool in her belly. Luca's eyes were glowing bright blue and she knew he was as aroused as she was but she was aware they were out in the open and chuckled as he sat back and watched her, she could already see his fangs pressing on his bottom lip.

"Anyone could be watching us," she sighed as he pulled her towards him and lifted her onto his lap. She wound her arms around his neck and she breathed in his clean scent mixed with the smell of cut grass and fresh air.

"Then they can watch me kissing my girl," he said and she wrapped her arms tighter and kissed him back. She could feel the tips of his fangs on her tongue and her breath caught in her throat and she groaned.

Luca stood abruptly and walked to the horses,

touching each of them on the forehead and whispering to them and watched as they cantered back the way they had come, back towards the stables.

He lifted Sierra in his arms and ran back in the direction of the house, she closed her eyes and held on tight. She felt his heart beating against her chest and was very aware of the hardness of his body against hers. He was fast as the wind and she buried her face into his neck as he flew through the trees.

Neither of them sensed the third presence watching them from high in the treetops a little further away from the trail. Luca was used to his scent in and around the estate so he would find nothing amiss if he stumbled across it.

He felt a flash of envy so strong as he watched them together that he surprised himself, he wanted her and he would have her one way or another, before he was forced to kill her.

CHAPTER TWENTY

Luca

When Sierra told me about the dress she was going to wear, I sought out my mother and asked for her counsel. She explained to me that most human women have been dreaming about their wedding day since their childhood. I was annoyed at myself for not realizing that Sierra may feel she was missing out on some human right of passage. I asked my mother to plan a wedding, rather than a claiming ceremony but we would recite the claiming vows needed to seal our bond instead of the religious ones favored at a traditional wedding and she nodded her approval.

Her friends would be on board with my plans, I was sure, but I managed to talk to them all one by one and they all promised to keep my secret. She suspected I was keeping something hidden but I locked that part of my mind from her and her eyes sparkled as she tried in vain to get me to talk. She could be extremely persuasive and I almost capitulated a couple of times when she was naked and compliant in my arms.

I watched her now from a distance as she sparred with Kai and when she feigned a right sweep of her leg to topple him and went with a left, he stumbled and she tossed him on his ass, much to the delight of the other vampires watching. Rufus, Malik and Lazarus had been drafted in to keep a close eye on the women as the ceremony was only a couple of days away now. Kai jumped to his feet smiling and bowed to her and she took a seat as Darci took her place in the makeshift arena.

She wasn't as strong as Sierra but she had been gradually developing her psychic ability with my mother's help and she was able to accurately predict her opponent's moves which gave her a real advantage.

She and my brother Ronan had a deep, mutual respect and had developed a close friendship but I didn't know if there was anything more at this stage. He was very protective of her though and was watching from the branches of a tree in the distance. She darted behind Kai to the left as he moved to the right and jumped on his back, a grin on her face and her pale blonde hair swinging in the breeze. Kai threw up his arms in mock surrender and Daeron declared everyone finished for the day.

I walked towards Sierra and took her hands in mine, kissing her gently. She was disheveled and her hair had come loose from the long braid. She looked right at home with the belt of knives and I noticed she had others stuck in the side of her boots too. She grinned as I raised an eyebrow.

"Do you want to go for a walk," I asked her and she slipped her arm into mine as we walked around the lumberyard and the blacksmith's shop.

"Only to the house," she smiled "I desperately need to shower."

She spoke to several people on the way and Marcus, the wolf shifter's three children ran to her and she hugged them before they scarpered off again chasing each other through the trees. I watched her face as her eyes followed them and realized I had underestimated just how much Sierra belonged here. My people loved her, vampire, elf and fae alike and even the stern Marcus had a soft spot for her. Sierra brought out the good in everyone and my love for her had never been as strong.

I filled the tub with water and added a concoction of herbs that my mother had prepared for her to help ease her sore body. I left her there with Alya to help her and ran downstairs quickly gathering the others together to make sure we were prepared and everyone knew what was expected of them for the wedding.

Greer assured me that Sierra didn't suspect anything and everything was falling into place nicely. Mother had prepared a charm to prevent Sierra from wanting to go near the ballroom in the next couple of days and Alya and Isadora would tie her up for the best part of tomorrow, leaving the rest of us free to finish the preparations.

Her friends wanted to spend this evening with her, a sort of makeshift bachelorette party, apparently something humans indulged in before marriage and I wanted her to have this experience too. The kitchen staff had prepared her favorite foods and were setting up a bar in the sunroom for the women to have this night together.

When I knew everything was under control I went back to our rooms and Sierra was laying on the bed fast asleep in her robe. I removed the remains of the sandwich and coffee Alya had brought for her earlier and lay down beside her, drawing her to my side and just watched her sleep.

Her thick, dark eyelashes were fanned out on her cheeks and her full lips were slightly parted. She had a soft golden glow to her skin and her blonde hair was streaked with paler silver lights, thanks to the weeks of training outside in the sunshine. I felt something stir in my gut and I couldn't wait until I claimed her. I wanted the world to know that she belonged to me and me to her.

She began to stir and she whispered my name in her sleep and I did something I haven't done in a while. I stripped off my clothes quickly and held her again as I closed my eyes and entered her dreams. She welcomed me immediately and I could see her smile as she reached up and touched my face. We were both naked and I lightly reached up and circled her breasts with my hands as she leaned her head back and sighed with pleasure. Her hands went to my hips and she pulled me towards her until she felt my arousal against her belly and she sucked in a breath.

"Luca," she sighed and I eased her onto her back and kneeled between her legs. I explored her body with my tongue, she tasted of honey and I knew I would never, ever get enough of her. I trailed my tongue down over her stomach and lifted her hips towards me as I slipped my tongue between her folds and gently sucked on her. I felt her hands fist in my hair and she pleaded with me to come to her. I teased her a little more before I slipped out of our dream.

She reached for me in her sleep and when I felt her fighting to wake I opened her robe and kneeled between her legs again and continued where we left off in the dream. She writhed and bucked towards me and dug her hands into my head as she arched off the bed, her eyes now open and watching me. I circled my finger on her sensitive nub as I kissed her inner thigh and felt my fangs lengthen in anticipation. I was rock hard and waited until the moment she started to whimper, to bite her inner thigh and sucked, as she lost her head completely and cried out, the waves crashed over her and I sealed the bite and entered her as she was still keening. She bucked against me and I came hard and fast as she clung to me and we rode the waves together.

I cradled her in my arms and felt her heartbeat gradually slow to match mine, I needed this woman more than I needed my next breath, no words were necessary.

CHAPTER TWENTY-ONE

Sierra

Sierra walked into the library with Luca and her friends were already there waiting for her with a fully stocked bar and an abundance of foodstuffs laid out on the tables. Brynna pushed a glass of bubbly into her hand and chased Luca out the door with a grin.

"No men allowed," she chastised,

"I'm a vampire, not a man," he grinned,

"No males allowed then," she laughed pushing him out the door.

She was surprised and very touched that they would do this for her and Brynna grinned and told her it was Luca that set it all up. Sorcha put on some music and they filled their plates with chicken, pasta and pizza and sat in a circle on the floor with their glasses full and toasted her. She had grown very close to these four women in the last few weeks and soon each of them would be planning a claiming ceremony too.

The wine loosened their lips and they each told their story of where they had come from and how they had met their mates. Sierra knew that Violette had a hand, using suggestion to get the women where they needed to be to meet her sons and it was working fine until the threat escalated and Sorcha and Darci had to be brought quicker than she had anticipated before she had a chance to situate them closer to the others. They met Ronan and Aeric for the first time the day they were brought to the House but were adjusting well under the circumstances.

As the alcohol flowed, they teased her mercilessly about Luca and after a few glasses she admitted that their sex life was amazing and raised her glass with a giggle as the others cheered and laughed.

Greer smiled and Brynna was all over her asking about her and Ettore. She looked around at their expectant faces and flushed as they cheered her when she told them that she found him incredibly hot but their relationship was still chaste. Darci and Ronan were rarely apart but she admitted they hadn't yet had sex. He was attentive and sweet and they spent all of their time together but she said apart from kissing her...nothing. The other women were unsure what to say but Brynna burst out laughing

"You need to seduce him Darc. Go upstairs tonight, put on your sexiest lingerie and seduce him. Don't take no for an answer." She reached for a bottle of champagne, stuck it in the ice bucket and passed it over.

"This will be chilled by the time you go to bed," she grinned at her friend and handed her two glasses.

Sorcha was eating her third plate of food, it was common for shifters to eat a lot, but she refused to be baited. She admitted she and Aeric too had come close but no sex.

"I am part wolf shifter and if I lose my head with him and bite him during sex and he bites me back, drawing blood, we will be bonded forever. I'm good with that," she admitted, her face flushing, "But I want to be absolutely sure that he is too," He was still sleeping in a guest room for now but Sierra thought they were perfect for each other.

Brynna jumped up then to change the music and

Sierra grinned at the distraction tactic. She so *did not* want to discuss Finn with anyone and she let it go for now. She was very curious however what had happened when he had thrown her over his shoulder and marched upstairs with her. Sierra thought it was kind of hot. She pushed the image into Brynnas mind and the petite girl sat cross legged on the floor and answered her aloud.

"It was hot, or it could have been if I hadn't locked him out on the balcony!" she grinned but refused to elaborate. They were certainly an interesting couple.

They felt the party start to naturally wind down and Sierra was a little tipsy. Darci handed them all a vial and she drunk it and felt herself quickly sober up. Before they headed upstairs, she wanted to say something to the other women as they may not get the chance again and this room had been charmed to shield their conversations from even their mates ears.

"When you come to the claiming ceremony, please make sure you have a weapon to defend yourselves with, on your person if possible or hidden in the room, I have an awful feeling something really bad is going to happen," she said and they all nodded in agreement.

"I thought the same thing Sierra" Greer said softly, "We have all taken steps but you need to worry about the ceremony and nothing else," she added making her promise.

Sierra hugged them all one last time and opened a link to Luca, who appeared instantly to take her upstairs to bed.

CHAPTER TWENTY-ONE

Luca

After living for over two hundred years and having faced countless challenges in my time, I have to admit that I am more than a little nervous. I love Sierra more than my life, she is my bonded, my soul, so why do I feel like she is hiding something from me. We have a permanent mental link but she can shield me for privacy and I would never insist otherwise, but she has been constantly shielding me for days now and although I have been doing the same with her it is only because I don't want to spoil the surprise of the wedding. Maybe it's nothing and I am just super sensitive to her just now, but I worry nonetheless.

I watched her train for a while this morning and although the sword is not her weapon of choice and she dismissed it at first, she handles it efficiently and I was intrigued watching her parry with the trainers. She can also handle a bow pretty accurately but Greer is the undisputed expert in that area. My brother watches her constantly, almost obsessively and I know Greer is aware of this but she doesn't really acknowledge him there.

After lunch, my mother sent Sierra off for makeup and hair trials leaving me free to finish the preparations for our wedding without fear of discovery.

The ballroom was awash with flowers. Masses of hydrangeas, peonies and roses covered every surface, the smell was intoxicating, and mother had charmed them to stay perfectly fresh until tomorrows ceremony. The two hundred or so chairs had been set out to resemble the aisle in a typical human wedding and candles surrounded the room and the staging area where we would pledge our bond and repeat our vows. They would be lit minutes before our guests arrived.

We set an area off to one side of the room where the musicians would assemble for the party afterward and I was dearly hoping Sierra loved what she saw.

I felt bad for her that she had no family left, but even if she did, we couldn't risk humans coming here. We are all capable of controlling our urges to feed and we have never taken without consent (Loosely implied consent in Finn's case) but others do not have the same moral standards as our house and it's too much of a risk.

I closed the doors again, locking it with a little magic, everything in here was perfect and went to find my father to see if he had any more news.

We now knew from a spy of our own that one of the ringleaders was the second son of another ancient house about a hundred miles from here. His name is Draven Demetrius and his father is a powerful and important vampire called Alessandro.

They have not moved at all with the times and they did not approve of my father's plans for us to mate with non-vampires but the council had approved it and although Alessandro was accepting, he was not terribly happy. Draven however, was furious. We have no evidence that his father was involved in any plot but Alessandro and his mate would be here as guests at the wedding and he would be watched very carefully. Draven and his mate had declined our invitation to come as had

Nikolai, Alessandro's oldest son and heir.

My father had arranged for plenty of extra security. Daeron had called on some of the elf community to help and they would be disguised as waiting and bar staff for the event.

Other vampires often foolishly dismissed the elves as non-threatening. On the whole, they were a peace loving, nonviolent people. But there were always exceptions. I chuckled though as I thought of Daeron, he was a warrior as fierce as I had ever known and as loyal to us as any. Alys and Alya were his daughters and his wife Calathiel was our healer, a gifted doctor with a traditional medical school degree but also the best magical healer I had ever known.

I walked to my mother's suite and knocked on the door before entering. She was kneeling in front of a small glass table, mixing powders and crumbling herbs into a small bowl. I waited until she looked up and her face stretched into a broad smile as she rose and came towards me.

"Luca, my son," she embraced me, "You are

troubled? Her smooth brow wrinkled with motherly concern.

"Mother, I am a little worried about Sierra. She has been shielding me from something and I have an awful feeling about it,"

She guided me to sit with her on the sofa and took my hands as she watched my face.

"I won't break through her defenses Luca," she shook her head "That would be a terrible violation of her privacy, she is as entitled to her innermost thoughts as you are son,"

"I know she is. I am just sick with the thought of her being hurt." I sighed and stood up to pace the room. Mother watched me with a smile on her face.

"Luca, don't make the mistake of underestimating Sierra. She is so much stronger than you know, give her a little credit,"

"But she is still human, she is vulnerable to our kind," I was sounding desperate but my mother wouldn't budge an inch.

"Talk to her son, tell her how you feel, I am sure

Sierra would not want to cause you anguish," she urged me and I knew I had no other choice but to do as she asked.

CHAPTER TWENTY-TWO

Sierra

She was sitting on the bed dressed in cotton shorts and a tank top and painting her toes a shimmering pale pink when Luca slipped quietly into the room. Her hair was still damp and bundled on top of her head and even scrubbed free of makeup she was still stunningly beautiful, he thought.

He watched her for a moment before she sensed him and looked up, a smile lighting her face as she held out her hand for him. She was still shielding him and he nudged her with his mind as he walked towards her. She ignored his request and smiled and patted the bed beside her as she stretched out her legs to dry her nails. She was definitely hiding something from him and as yet hadn't fully learned to compartmentalize her thoughts so that she could hide some and be open with others.

He kicked off his shoes and sat up beside her on the

bed, pulling her back to lean on him and he drank in her scent, his heart filling with love.

"Why are you shielding me, Sierra," he asked abruptly as the fear clutched his heart again and he had to know what she was hiding from him.

She turned to look at him, her amethyst eyes flickered with hurt,

"Am I not entitled to my private thoughts Luca, you told me before that you would always respect that,"

He heaved a sigh and run his hand through his hair before he spoke again, trying hard to remain calm.

"You are and I do my love, I am just worried about you, I want you to be safe Sierra and with the ceremony being so close now," he tailed off imploring her to understand.

She smiled as she raised her hand to his face and stroked the stubble she found so incredibly sexy on him.

"You have been shielding me too Luca, what is it you're hiding from me," She caught him off guard and he laughed then and she raised her eyebrows waiting for him to answer.

"It's only to do with the ceremony my love, I promise," he said and she pulled herself onto his lap to face him and he wrapped his arms around her waist. "I wanted to do something nice to surprise you. It is a good surprise,"

"Me too" she grinned, "I promise it's a good thing and nothing for you to worry about," she said, still smiling and he relaxed a little as she leaned in and kissed him.

As usual, all rational thought left his head as he tightened his grip and felt the heat engulf him as they kissed. She affected him like no one ever had and he felt himself grow hard with just the slightest touch from her.

He groaned as he slipped his hands inside the tank top and felt the heat from her skin scorch his hands. He heard her heart hammering in her chest and he flipped her over onto her back and pulled the top over her head. Capturing her nipple in his mouth, he bit down and she gasped as she pushed her hips against his rock-hard length and she wrapped her legs around his waist. He reached between them and tore her shorts in two in his hurry and leaned back to drink in the sight of her naked body.

"You are so incredibly beautiful Sierra," he whispered as he watched her,

Her eyes were misty and her lips swollen and he wanted to bury himself deep inside her. Impatiently he pulled off his shirt and she stilled his hands when he reached for his jeans.

"Wait," she smiled, "Allow me,"

He stood still as she slid to the edge of the bed and without touching him she started to chant quietly to herself and reached a hand towards him, stopping short a foot from where he stood, and he watched in amazement as the button on his jeans snapped open and the zipper slid all the way down.

"How?" he questioned and she was cut off from answering as he shook his head and kicked off his clothes and came towards her, covering her body with his.

He pushed it out of his mind as his emotions overtook him and he gathered her to him and she wrapped herself around him, aroused and ready. He thrust inside her and she opened a tiny part of her mind to him, showing him what she wanted and he complied with her wishes. In only a few minutes he felt her muscles tense as she screamed out loud and he bit into the delicate, soft skin of her neck, pulling only a little blood, just enough to intensify her feelings. He wanted her to be as strong as possible tomorrow. She called out again and he muffled her screams with his mouth and he thrust one last time, calling her name over and over.

They collapsed on the bed and she lay across him, her smile still in place as her heart slowed down to normal and she thanked the goddess for Luca, she hadn't even lived until she met him.

CHAPTER TWENTY-THREE

Luca

Apparently, I was being banished to a guest room for the evening as it's unlucky to see the bride the night before the wedding. I wanted to point out to Brynna that this was technically a claiming ceremony and we had no such childish superstition but relented at her stubborn refusal to change her mind and moved some things into one of the empty rooms down the hallway.

I took some comfort from the fact that Sierra was as unhappy with the arrangement as I was. I kissed her goodbye as her friends and Alya watched, waiting to whisk her away to prepare her for tomorrow. I grimaced at the thought, she was already beautiful and needed no help in that department. I spent a miserable night without her curled up in my arms and was so glad it would be the last one.

My mother insisted that we all fortify ourselves with

bags of human blood before the ceremony to make us as strong as possible. It also sharpens our senses and we needed every advantage we could get. We didn't want to draw from our mates which could weaken them a little as we needed them to also be as strong as possible, even if it was to run and hide as we had instructed them. That was the plan for them if things were to go wrong.

There was a safe room behind the ballroom, my father had the room converted when we knew the women would be coming here to protect them in the event of an attack. The heavy steel door was disguised by the stage curtains and without the code to get in, could only be opened from the inside. Sierra knew where it was and would guide her friends there if things turned ugly.

I wrinkled my nose in disgust as I drank the chilled blood given to me by mother. Compared to the sweet, honeyed taste of my bonded's blood it tasted bitter and foreign. Ettore had a similar expression on his face and I wondered if he had been sampling Greer's blood too or if he was just being his usual fastidious self.

We also had breakfast with our parents as human food

also fortified us up to a point. I saw Alys and Alya carrying trays of waffles and bacon and a pot of coffee to our suite and I knew the other women would make sure Sierra ate something before the ceremony.

The guests were starting to arrive and Daeron nodded to me that everyone was in place. I saw a lot of elves and even a few fae that I did not recognize but I trusted Daeron to choose the right people. They mingled among the guests, handing out appetizers, some of the vampire guests ate human food and some did not but they were all happy to take a glass of champagne or wine.

I noticed two men in the corner, dressed appropriately in tuxedos but I could smell the wolf in them. I nudged Daerons mind and asked about them and he answered that they were brothers of Marcus. Looking closely, I could see the resemblance and I was glad of their presence. Shifters were incredibly strong, fierce fighters and we needed all the protection we could get. I nodded to them and got a slight inclination of the head from the taller of the two.

The room was filling up fast and at last, I saw

Alessandro come into the ballroom and take a seat. My mother watched him closely and I could see no hint of concern on her face, she was adept at rooting out malice and intent in others and for now, she looked satisfied.

Just when my blood pressure started to settle Draven came waltzing in too with his mate and his eyes scanned the room until they fell on me and he smirked before taking a seat. I felt the anger coursing through my veins and I wanted to snap his neck. I knew by his expression he was up to something but he was heavily shielded. I felt my fathers gaze and I turned to him to see him shake his head and grimace. I knew I could do nothing yet but I would be watching him, I forced my anger down and kept a neutral expression on my face.

I mingled and spoke to friends and saw Daeron at the back of the room, his keen eyes were constantly scanning but they kept falling back to Draven, I was a little easier knowing Daeron was watching him closely.

At my father's request, everyone took their seats and the light classical music playing in the background changed to a more somber beat. I walked to the door as

Sierra's friends came in one by one, all dressed in knee-length dresses in pale pink chiffon and took their place on the opposite side of the dais from my brothers. I saw Finn openly appraise Brynna and earned a sour look in return. Beautiful women each and every one but I had only one woman on my mind.

I opened the door a little wider and my breath caught in my throat as I caught my first glimpse of my mate.

She was dressed like a human bride in a beautiful white lace dress that fit her body perfectly, leaving her back bare and her hair was adorned with white rosebuds. I had never seen her look more stunning and my heart was doing somersaults as she walked towards me. Her eyes were huge in her face and I thought I saw her lip tremble and I wanted so much to sweep her into my arms. She was flanked by two guards and they blended into the crowd as I held out my hand.

Alya and Alys grinned at my expression and I moved aside to let them take their seats as I took my bonded's hand in mine and we walked slowly down the aisle for our ceremony. I saw her bite her bottom lip to stop the trembling and I squeezed her hand as she met my eyes and I saw happiness shining there too. I was discreetly scanning the guests for signs of trouble but so far nothing was out of place and we reached the front and climbed onto the dias and faced each other, holding hands. There were also two members of the council there to witness the joining.

My father, as head of our House, performed the binding ceremony where we each had to pledge our love, honor and eternal protection to the other halves of our heart and soul and to our House. It would be expected that Sierra would eventually become like me but there was no timeline only the promise that someday it would be so.

The ceremony bound her not only to me but to our House which should have afforded her protection within the council's laws but because she was not yet a vampire there were plenty who would ignore the law as they deemed her beneath us. The thought made my anger raw.

I took a dagger from my belt and raised Sierra's hand and nicked her just enough to allow a few drops of her blood to drip into the chalice and sealed the cut with my tongue, she tasted sweeter than ever. I then sliced my own hand to offer to her. She took it in both hands as she watched the crimson drops spill into the cup to mingle with her own and then she put it to her lips and tasted me until my wound closed. She licked the red droplets from her lips and I knew she would be just a little stronger from sampling my blood.

As my father recited the last words of the ceremony, I mixed a little wine into the chalice and we each drank from it to complete our bond. As we walked down from the dais and the band started to play, I swung her into my arms and kissed her.

"There is no going back now my love, you are bonded to me for eternity," I teased her when I raised my head and she leaned into me with a satisfied smile on her lips.

"And you to me, Luca, forever," she smiled.

Her friends crowded around her and dragged her off to the bar as my brothers joined me watching them depart. I noticed Daeron himself trailing Sierra and I was glad of his dedication. He was a fearsome sight, standing a few inches taller than me with a permanently emotionless expression on his proud face, his long braids trailing down his back.

Ettore handed me a glass of champagne and just as I started to relax there was a commotion from the far side of the room and I saw Draven pushing Malik, one of the vampires on our security detail, against the wall. He was shouting, spit coming from his mouth and I quickly crossed the room and clamped my hand on his shoulder as he whirled round to face me. I was much stronger than him and he knew it. I put my other hand up to stop Malik attacking him.

"Oh look who it is, the dirty little human lover,"

"I think it would be best if you left now Draven," I said, grinding my teeth as I dug my fingers painfully into his shoulder. It took everything in me to not snap the vampire's neck. "You have insulted me, my bonded and our House with your display, you are no longer welcome here,"

He started to shout obscenities and only stopped when his father approached and quietly ordered him to leave.

He shook off my hand and marched out, Malik on his tail to make sure he left the grounds of the estate and not just the house.

Alessandro apologized and bowed his head but I could see the fury in his eyes as he followed his son. He may not agree with our bonding but he was a stickler for etiquette and manners and Draven had embarrassed him tonight.

I glanced towards Sierra and she raised her glass to me and I relaxed. With Draven finally out of the way, we could enjoy the rest of our day without worry.

CHAPTER TWENTY-FOUR

Sierra

Sierra looked across the ballroom at the fearsome expression on Luca's face and shivered. When he was angry he looked like every inch of the formidable predator that she knew him to be. The thought didn't scare her though as she knew she was safe with Luca in every single way.

When she had tasted his blood at the ceremony, she had felt the strength of their bond and the power and energy in her muscles. She knew even a little of his blood would make her stronger but she didn't realize it would be instant.

When Draven was escorted from the house by one of the vampire guards, she felt a shift in the mood and atmosphere and raised her glass to Luca to let him know she was okay.

He joined her and he insisted on piling a plate high

188

with food for her and they sat at one of the tables by the window. She ate some chicken and smoked salmon just to appease him. Luca didn't eat but he took another glass of wine from a passing waiter and watched her as she surprisingly finished the meal.

The chairs in the middle of the floor had been quickly cleared and he swept her onto the dance floor and she leaned into him as they swayed to the music. She could feel the eyes of the others on her and she picked up different moods from them, ranging from curiosity to disapproval.

She noticed a beautiful, dark-haired vampire watching her closely and she felt a surge of hatred before the feeling was cut short and she knew the woman was shielding her emotions.

She opened her mouth to tell Luca when she was suddenly yanked viciously backward, out of his arms and she felt the pressure of cold, hard, steel against her throat. The vampire who held her also had a vice grip on her arm and she winced in pain as he dragged her away from her mate.

The ballroom fell silent and she heard a gasp from Greer.

Luca looked murderous but he didn't try to approach them as he knew, as did she, that he would slit her throat in an instant. She could feel the stench of contempt and hostility emanating from her captor and she opened her mind just a little to allow her fear to seep out. The vampire behind her let loose an ugly laugh as he smelled the fear but she felt his grip relax just a little as he gauged, she posed no threat to him. She watched Lucas face and opened up to him, telling him what she was going to do.

He screamed in her head "NO Sierra" but she pretended to faint dead away and the vampire still held her arm in a grip but removed the knife from her throat, waving it in the air as he backed them against the wall.

Sierra's hand was by her side and as Luca held the vampire's attention, demanding he let her go, she slipped her hand into the zipper holding the bottom part of her dress on and stealthily pulled out a small knife from the sheath attached to her leg.

She moaned as she turned, making her captive look at her as she dangled from his hand, before dismissing her as irrelevant and looking back to Luca, and she struck.

She raised the knife quickly and slashed the arm holding her which made him release her with a roar and she dropped to the floor, rolling away from him. Turning the knife quickly in her hand she threw it with deadly accuracy into his stomach. He howled with pain but came at her again and Luca blocked him and took him down. Finn ran towards his brother and sh-e watched as Luca heard his brothers shout and caught the sword Ettore threw at him and sliced the vampires head from his body in one stroke.

Sierra scrambled to her feet and quickly unzipping the bottom of her dress so that she could move easier as she looked to her friends who were watching the scene in horror. She saw Greer move quickly behind the curtain and returned with her bow in her hand, jumping high up onto the dais, her keen eyes scanning the crowd for further trouble. Ettore shouted to Kai and Toran to protect the women and they were beside them in a flash.

Another vampire she didn't know rushed at Luca but Ronan tackled him to the ground and Finn and Ronan dragged him from the room. She turned to Luca again as three vampires started to come at him and she pulled three of her knives without thinking and threw them. One hit the first vampire in the cheek and he fell to the ground where Violette bound him with magic and he screamed and struggled to get free until she chanted something more and he fell silent.

The second and third knife hit the second vampire in the chest and stomach and Hendrik lifted him like he was weightless and snapped his neck. Luca easily stopped the third and Violette again bound him and he was dragged away, she sensed from Luca they would be held for questioning.

Sierra straightened and felt for the knives strapped to the other leg aware that the guests were watching her with interest. She thought the fight was over and Luca was making his way towards her when the dark-haired woman that had been watching her earlier let out an animalistic scream and ran towards her, her face was twisted with loathing.

She was so fast she didn't have time to throw a knife and put out her hands to brace herself for the impact. The vampire dropped right in front of her and Sierra saw the arrow sticking out of her back and the large pool of blood seeping out from under her body. Sweet, brave Greer had saved her life, she had shot the vampire straight through her rotten heart.

Hendrik ordered his security to take the women to their rooms. He intended to find out who among the guests left in the ballroom were enemies, by whatever means possible. Sierra nudged her friend's minds to gather in her room, there is safety in numbers and together they stood a better chance of protecting themselves.

"Luca I will need you and your brothers,"

Luca didn't look happy about leaving her as the other women were ushered away and held her tightly in his arms but Malik took her arm and bowed to him.

"I will make sure she is safe Luca, let her come with me,"

He released her with a sigh and they left the ballroom quickly, her friends already on their way upstairs to safety.

They hurried through the hallway but when they reached the bottom of the stairs, Malik pulled her quickly towards the front door and she suddenly felt uneasy with him.

"We are to stay in my suite," Sierra reminded him as she began to feel uneasy as she reached for a knife, but the vampire lifted a hand and hit her hard on the side of the head and she saw the evil grin spread across his face just before everything went black.

CHAPTER TWENTY-FIVE

Luca

I could feel my fury threatening to take over as we weeded out seven more vampires among our guests who showed their true colors under my father's persuasive questioning. They were taken to the basement to be held for the council, where we had cells, charmed and bound by magic, they would not escape. The other guests were allowed to leave, some offered to stay and help but we didn't need them. I was desperate to go to Sierra but I needed to talk to my parents and brothers first.

Daeron was questioning the first of our prisoners and it looked like there were a lot more of our kind involved that we had originally thought. The council would not approve of our methods of extracting information but for once I did not care how he got the information. The two witnesses quickly left to inform the council what had happened here tonight and would gather back here tomorrow morning to question them for themselves.

I thought about my mate. My heart had almost stopped when the vampire, whose name escapes me, another from the House of Demetrius, held that knife to her throat. I thought I would lose her before our lives together had barely begun and she surprised me yet again with her courage when she stabbed him and threw the knife at his stomach. She stopped another two vampires from killing me too, she would be fearsome as a vampire with the added strength and speed she would gain. More importantly, she would be safe as a vampire, no longer hunted and I knew that having children was no longer a priority for me, keeping Sierra safe was all that mattered. I would talk to her tonight about changing her immediately, I only hoped she could see it my way because I knew I was asking a lot from her.

I quickly ran upstairs when we finished our meeting, needing to hold her, feel her close to me. A young vampire guard was outside the door to our suite and I nodded to him as I opened the door and went inside. Greer came rushing to meet me

"Where is Sierra, she didn't come upstairs with the rest of us," she asked and I felt my stomach plummet and the blood drain from my face as I realized in an instant she had been taken. I felt sick to my stomach for the first time since I was changed more than two hundred years ago and I threw open the door and flew downstairs to my father's study.

He was still there with my brothers when I went in and I told him quickly what had happened.

"Malik took her," I gasped as the pain threatened to overwhelm me and my father took my arm. "He was supposed to protect her and he took her, I will rip the beating heart from his fucking chest."

My mother entered the study and she already knew what happened as I had pushed the events into her mind as I ran downstairs.

"I will look for her son," she said softly as she hurried out again and we followed her to her rooms where she carried out her spells. She knelt at the glass table and repeated the incantation over and over again as she held an amulet in her hand and blew on the mixed powders in her hand, scattering them throughout the room.

Her power was awesome to behold and I felt the rise in energy and felt the air pulse as her skin turned iridescent and her hair lifted softly as if there were a breeze in the room. The white stone in the amulet turned orange and she chanted Sierra's name over and over before she closed her eyes for a moment and the energy in the room returned to normal. Her eyes snapped open again and she looked up at me.

"Whoever is behind this Luca has a very powerful witch working with them and I cannot see where she is being held. She held out the amulet on a chain. This will guide you as you get closer to her son and I will keep trying to locate her. They will probably have taken her far enough away that she cannot contact you with her mind, although I doubt that they even know yet what she is capable of.

I left the room and hurried to the car. I would need it for her when I found her, I had to find her, I just couldn't see it any other way. My brothers ran behind me and I didn't resist when they insisted on coming with me. My father was going to 'persuade' the prisoners to tell what they knew or he would execute them one by one, I was only sorry I would not be there to witness it myself.

As I sped through the night towards the House of Demetrius the amulet remained the same cold white color, but I had to start somewhere.

CHAPTER TWENTY-SIX

Sierra

Sierra felt nauseous, the dull pain in the side of her head forced her into consciousness, but she forced her breathing to stay even and kept her eyes closed. She didn't know if she was alone and wanted time to scope out where she was before her captors realized she was awake.

She suspected Malik the instant he tried to pull her towards the front door but she had been too slow to act. He had knocked her unconscious before she had a chance to grab a knife from the sheath on her leg. She now knew it would have been smarter to have played along and called out through her link for Luca but she had acted on the spur of the moment and felt foolish for it now.

She didn't sense anyone with her and opened her eyes slowly. She was laying on the middle of a bed but her wrists and ankles were tightly bound to the posts and she could barely move.

She pulled on the restraints but they didn't budge an inch. She was still wearing her dress, with the bottom part removed and her feet were bare but her knives and sheath had been taken from her.

She looked around frantically, trying to think of any way to escape when the door opened and Malik came into the room. He smiled as he came towards her but it didn't reach the madness of his eyes and he sat down on the bed and reached out to run his hand up the length of her leg to her thigh, caressing her skin and she struggled fruitlessly against him as he laughed maniacally.

"Struggle as much as you want little rabbit, it only makes the catch all the sweeter," he laughed again and she felt a cold dread settle beside the nausea in the pit of her stomach.

"Just kill me and get it over with," she said coldly.

He reached over, his face inches from hers and smiled,

"I intend to, little rabbit. But first I am going to sample what you give out so freely and so often to Luca, heir apparent," he sneered at the last part of his statement before he touched his lips to hers and she felt nothing but revulsion course through her body.

She struggled uselessly against him but he held her face roughly and continued to kiss her, pushing his tongue through her lips.

"I am going to kill you beautiful," he stated matter of factly as he leaned back and squeezed her breasts painfully and she shuddered. "But the manner of your death will be entirely dependent on how 'Nice' you are to me. If I have to fight you every inch of the way while I take your body then I will kill you slowly and painfully, although a little struggle is a turn on," he smiled evilly again "However if you were to make sure I enjoy it, then I will make your death painless and quick."

She refused to look at him but he yanked her head to his and she saw the demented look in his red glowing eyes and his fangs were fully extended and sharp. He grabbed her arm and put it to his lips and brushed his fangs over her skin. She shuddered and closed her eyes but he abruptly dropped it and stood up. As he opened the door he turned back,

"I will give you a little time to think about which way you are going to die, princess," and he left the room chuckling.

She wanted to cry but wouldn't give him the satisfaction and summoned up all the energy she could muster and opened her mind,

"Luca, help me please," she screamed in her head, "Malik is going to kill me," She projected the room around her. She had no idea where she was so she couldn't tell him but she didn't know what else to do. She didn't tell him about his other threats because it would enrage him and she needed him to have a clear head. She knew that Malik had probably taken her far enough away that she wouldn't be able to communicate but she had to do something. She pulled again on her arms but she was stuck firmly.

As her anger grew she could feel the heat radiating through her body and her fingertips felt like she was on fire. She wondered what was happening to her, had he given her something while she was asleep? The heat dissipated again before she had time to work out what it was.

An idea was beginning to form in her mind but she needed her hands free. She drew on all of her acting skills and when he came back into the room she forced a lone tear, letting it slide down her face. She knew he wouldn't be affected by tears but she wanted him to feel her resignation at her predicament, her acceptance of what was to come.

"So little rabbit, what's it to be," he asked as he stood in the doorway and removed his shirt. He was good-looking, like most vampires and looked like he worked out a lot, but he also had a wild, crazy look in his eyes.

She licked her lips and spoke softly to him,

"I don't want to die painfully Malik and you are kind of hot so I guess we do it your way," she smiled at him and he watched her for a while before he walked to the bed and gripped her thigh hard, running his hand along the bare skin of her leg.

"You're just a little human whore aren't you," he chuckled as he leaned over and scraped his fangs along her cheek. She could feel the revulsion rise up in her and forced it down, closing her eyes and moaning as he pulled her bottom lip down with his teeth and drew blood. He groaned as he tasted her blood and she looked at him through her lashes and knew he was reacting to her fake arousal.

He lay down beside her and kissed her again, softly, surprising her with how gentle he could be and she played it to her advantage. She forced herself to kiss him back, running her tongue across his lips as she moaned again and she felt his heart rate soar. She felt the bile rising in her throat and wanted so badly to pull away from him but forced herself to continue the charade and pushed her tongue inside his mouth. He grabbed her hair and pulled her lips hard against his, bruising the soft flesh as he probed with his tongue.

"Will you please release my arms," she begged him "I want to touch you, Malik," she said in her most sultry voice,

He leaned back to look at her and she held his gaze and smiled

"I can hardly run off if my feet are still bound and anyway you would catch me easily," she added as she bit her bottom lip until it turned bright red with blood and he watched her carefully before he reached up and snapped the restraints on her hands and reached down and did the same to her legs.

She felt the blood rush back to her limbs and sucked in a breath as her heart hammered in her chest at her good luck, she didn't expect him to release her legs as well.

She wrapped her arms around him as he nuzzled her neck and she stroked his back. She could feel his arousal plainly now and she needed to act quickly before he had a chance to violate her. She giggled playfully and rolled him off of her and sat astride his body and he grinned and reached up to rip her dress in two and discard it on the floor.

She was painfully aware that she wore no bra under her dress and his eyes feasted on her breasts as she swallowed and felt her hatred of him rise in her gut. If she was going to die at the hands of this monster it would be before he had a chance to touch her again. She also knew the minute she acted she had signed her death warrant and he would kill her instantly but she wanted to maim him before she went, give Luca a chance to kill him.

She smiled her best sexy smile as she reached up to unpin her hair, shaking her head to let the waves fall loosely around her face, she leaned over him and put her hand on his heart and giggled again as she felt the organ beat fast beneath her fingers.

"I may just keep you alive for a while longer little rabbit if you play this nicely all the time," he ground out as he reached for her breast and tore his nails downward through her flesh and watched her blood run in rivulets down her body.

His eyes blazed red and the heat flared through her at the searing pain he had inflicted and she mentally sent a message to Luca,

"I love you my darling," before she leaned forward as if to kiss him and slipped the tiny dagger she had removed from her hair and plunged it deep into his racing heart.

She felt the warm liquid spurt all over her nearly

naked body before she was violently thrown against the wall and her world went black.

CHAPTER TWENTY-SEVEN

Luca

We were speeding along the highway at over a hundred miles an hour when I felt the nudge in my mind and I heard her message

"Luca, help me please, Malik is going to kill me,"

I had no idea where he was keeping her but I turned the car and sped back the way we had come, instinctively knowing they were closer to home that I had first thought. I smacked my hand on the wheel at the many miles I had put between us already

I used a little magic to share her projection of the room she had shared with me where she was being held into my brother's mind's and Ettore swore,

"That's Greer's house, she's in Greer's bedroom,"

I put my foot down harder and was thankful to the goddess that the roads were quiet as we raced against time to reach her. My red hot anger had turned to a cold, single-minded determination to kill Malik very, very slowly, torturing him until he was begging for his life and then I would kill him anyway. I had known him for decades and although I didn't particularly like him I had thought him loyal to our house.

We were only a few minutes from Greer's old home when I had another message from Sierra telling me she loved me. She was completely closed to me so I couldn't reply and I choked back a sob as I prayed to the goddess it wasn't because she was already dead.

The amulet in my hand was growing more orange by the minute and

I swerved around corners at breakneck speed to reach her. Ettore put his hand on my arm warning me not to alert Malik to our arrival and to stop the car further along the road, away from the house.

I did as he asked and we slipped out into the fading light and noiselessly ran along the back of the gardens and into Greer's house through the kitchen door. Finn and Ronan did a perimeter search in case there were others here with Malik while the other two came with me.

I smelled the blood as soon as I opened the door and although it wasn't the strongest, I could smell Sierra's sweet scent among it. I followed my nose, my heart frozen in fear and burst in through the bedroom door. Malik was lying on the bed, almost dead, the blood pumping out of him so fast he would be gone in minutes. I recognized the tiny jeweled dagger sticking out of his chest as Sierra's and was glad she got to exact her revenge.

I took in the restraints on the bed and Maliks naked form and my mind thundered as I thought what he might have done to her. I rushed to the other side of the bed and I saw her lying on a heap on the floor, covered in blood and I roared in anguish as I gathered her to me and held her tight, I couldn't bear to think what had transpired in here tonight. I could feel a pulse and knew she was still alive as I carried her to the bathroom and tried to wash off the blood to see the extent of her injuries.

There was a lump on the side of her head and series of jagged cuts on her left breast and I winced as I thought how they might have occurred. I extended my fangs and bit into my wrist and let the blood flow over the cuts and watched as they closed and healed. I dripped a little blood into her mouth and rubbed her throat gently to encourage her to swallow, it would help her heal. I filled the basin with warm, soapy water and washed the blood from her skin. I didn't want her to wake and see his blood splattered all over her body.

I wrapped her gently in a towel and carried her downstairs. My brothers were cleaning the room as I passed and Malik's body was gone, in its place a pile of dark grey ash.

Ettore brought me some pajamas of Greers she had left behind and left me to dress her as he went outside to build a fire to destroy the bloodied clothes and mattress. He told me wordlessly that he had removed Malik's head from his body to ensure his death. I wrapped my arms around her and held her against me, rocking her in my arms until she started to come around.

She smiled when she saw me and reached up to touch my face. My brave, beautiful love.

"You came for me Luca," she said and my heart filled

with love as my bonded closed her eyes and whispered,
    "Take me home."

CHAPTER TWENTY-EIGHT

Sierra

Luca had hovered around her constantly for the next two days and Sierra knew they were going to have to talk about what happened. He hadn't said anything and was avoiding the conversation but she knew he feared the worst, that Malik had raped her.

Calathiel, the healer, had been to visit her and said there would be no lasting physical damage to her but she would have some mental scars from her attack. Sierra knew she would not let them win by being afraid, she was stronger than that.

She insisted Luca sit beside her on the bed and she took his hands in hers and implored him to listen to her. She could have shown him in her mind but she didn't think it would help in this instance for him to see the details of her abduction. She explained everything to him, even down to her pretending to go along with Malik and kissing him back to buy some time to formulate her plan. She felt him wince but he remained silent as she told her story, in full. When she had finished he buried his head in her hair and held her tightly, thanking the goddess for the thousandth time that she was safe.

He felt her breathing change and she pulled him down beside her and opened the buttons on his shirt, despite his protests that she needed to rest some more.

"What I need Luca, is you," she insisted and climbed on his lap to remove the shirt and throw it on the floor. She needed to wipe the experience with Malik from her mind and replace it with something precious and Luca was that and much more to her

Despite himself, he felt his arousal grow and he threaded his hands into her hair and kissed her as he pushed her onto her back to remove her clothes. She lay there naked and he felt his heart jolt as he realized how close he had come to losing her. He stripped quickly and covered her body with his as she welcomed him in and they made love slowly and tenderly until she urged him to bite her. He shied away from it because he wanted her to be strong again but she was insistent. She needed this from him to begin to heal.

"Please Luca, she begged until he finally broke the skin on her neck with his teeth and pulled on her. She instantly started to keen and the more he sucked the more intense her orgasm grew. She bit him back and he came with her, crying out and rocking into her until she slowed and lay spent with him on top of her.

He carried her to the shower and they cleaned up together, he washed her all over with a soft flannel, being very gentle with her, before he carried her back to bed and pulled her against him and ordered her to rest.

She looked like an angel as she slept with her golden hair falling around her beautiful face, but as he looked at her naked breasts, the skin was smooth and healed but he could still see the memory of the jagged marks of Malik's fingernails and the blood running from them. He pictured her tied to the bed with restraints and laying on the floor covered in her attacker's blood, and he felt sick to his stomach. He would need to talk to her in the morning, he knew she would probably resist him but he had to try and

216

convince her to let him change her.

She woke to the delicious smell of bacon and coffee and sat up in bed, pulling on her discarded tank top as Luca brought her breakfast. There was a plate of pancakes and a glass of orange juice as well and she was so hungry and ate most of it before she pushed the tray away and sipped on her coffee. She was attuned to Luca and knew he had something on his mind.

"Just spit it out," she smiled as he paced up and down in front of her in a pair of low-slung jeans and his chest bare. She wanted to run her hands along his defined muscles but snapped her mind back to him as he spoke.

"Sierra, I know we talked about you becoming like me after we had children and you agreed you would like to do that," she nodded and waited for him to continue. "I would like to change you now, I don't want to wait any longer," he blurted out and she put down her cup to look at him.

"No Luca," she said and he sat on the bed beside her, taking her hands,

"Sierra please, we have many more enemies than the

ones we have already caught and the only way I know you will be safe is if I change you," he pleaded with her but she was still shaking her head,

"Luca, I can't," she told him and he jumped up again,

"What do you mean you can't. Can't now or can't ever," he asked quietly and she saw him pale at the thought that she would never want to change despite their previous agreement.

"No Luca, I can't right now," she tried to explain but he cut her off again,

"Sierra, you promised you would want this, I know we said we would have children first but sweetheart it's just too risky, waiting to see who else will try and hurt you. I am going out of my mind here!"

"No Luca, I can't let you change me just now because I am already pregnant," she said reaching up to touch his face, "Calathiel confirmed it, It's what I have been shielding from you for the last couple of weeks. We're going to have a baby."

She watched the shocked expression on his face turn to joy and knew she had made the right decision. She could feel Luca's baby growing inside of her and it was the most wonderful feeling in the world.

To Be Continued...

Turn the page and read on for a glimpse into Greer and Ettore's story in Vampire Brides - From This Day Forward.

Yvonne x

VAMPIRE BRIDES

From This Day Forward

PROLOGUE

Ettore

I know Greer is still a little unsure of 'us' and although she has watched Luca and Sierra bonding and falling in love she still has her reservations about this whole process and about me. I think me following her for weeks before we met freaked her out a little, which I understand, but it's what I knew I had to do to win my mate over.

It would have been difficult to knock on her door, introduce myself as a vampire and ask her for a date. I chuckled at the thought. I think however she is most annoyed at me for invading what she thought were private dreams and baring her soul to me as well as her body. I had never in all my years seen anything as exquisite as Greer's naked body.

I had wooed her intimately in our dreams for weeks and had tasted and touched every part of her mind and body before I had to render her unconscious and she was forcibly brought to our House for her own protection.

When she gained consciousness, she realized I wasn't a stranger to her after all and she was furious. I had planned to make myself known to her that very same night but after I kidnapped her she shut me out of my room and I never got the chance. I am not sure however if she is angry at me or at herself because she enjoyed the intimacy in our dreams as much as I had. Although I obviously wasn't stupid enough to point this out to her.

Greer is half elf and has suspected from a young age what she is, although she had no kin to speak of, so is still unaware of the strength of her gifts. She is also not hung up on nudity as most humans can be, and that fact is staring me in the face as she stands with her hands on her hips, frowning at me as naked as the day she was born.

I am trying really hard to concentrate on what she is saying, but staring at her smooth pale skin and her lovely face, the blood has suddenly escaped my head and has made for another part of my anatomy as I gaze upon her beautiful body. Despite all of this we have become quite close and I have kissed her many times which she seems to enjoy.

"Ettore," she raises her voice a little, my name sounds like a caress on her tongue, "Are you listening to me?"

"I really am trying Greer," I grind out, "But you are making it extremely difficult standing there like that," I gestured to her and she threw up her arms in disgust and walked off into the bathroom, my eyes were glued to her firm ass and her long, long legs.

I want to strip naked and follow her, bend her over and sink deep into her beautiful body, I am so hard I think it might break off but instead I stomp out of the room and resign myself to another night in the guest room and a long, cold shower. I think of all the ways to try and make her understand but when she is in front of me, I lose all reason and I blubber like a weak-minded fool. I may go insane if I don't have her soon!

The sheets feel cool on my skin and I lay for the longest time with my arms above my head, staring into the darkness, thinking of Greer. I haven't been able to think about anything but her since I first set eyes on her.

When my mother and father laid out their plans for us to mate with humans I was dead set against it from the start, adamant I would choose my own mate when the time was right. Luca was also on my side but as soon as he saw his mate, Sierra, he was hooked and I was left to battle our father on my own. Eventually, it was seeing Luca and Sierra together that convinced me that maybe my mother was right and had found my bonded after all. I would at least go to Greer and watch her.

I was entranced from the first moment but I held back from any contact with her, just watching from a distance, until Luca caught me hiding in a tree, watching her house. He convinced me to go to her in a shared dream and I had. I felt my mouth tug up in a smile at the memory and my fangs growing long in my mouth.

At first, it had been magical, an incredible experience and she had opened up to me and I to her. We talked for hours and when I first kissed her she was receptive and warm. In our shared dream, we were intimate the night before I was forced to kidnap her and although it was wonderful it left me wanting more. I wanted the real thing, to feel her warm body beneath my fingertips and bury my head in the sweet lavender and vanilla scent of her hair. I needed to hold her warm flesh in my arms as she cried out my name and I buried myself deep inside her.

I would talk to her again in the morning. I have an idea that I think she may be receptive to. Greer is a trained nurse and although she can't go back to the job at the hospital, I think I know something that will help her settle here with us. I will take her and introduce her to Calathiel soon. She has been our healer for decades and would welcome any help Greer could give her at the estate clinic.

We were trying to get back to some semblance of normalcy in our house after Sierra was abducted and almost died at her and Luca's claiming ceremony a few weeks ago. We caught some of the vampires involved and executed them. The council had the others at their headquarters and it didn't bode well for them. We knew

Draven Demetrius, son of another powerful House of vampires was at least one of the ring leaders but as yet no one would implicate him.

My mother, an extremely powerful witch before she became a vampire, is convinced there is someone else behind this too. She believes, however, that for the next few days at least, the women are safe, no one would risk another attack when the council are actively sniffing around the estate.

I was balancing on the edge of sleep when I heard a slight noise, it was my bedroom door creaking open. In the darkness, my keen sight saw her standing on the threshold, undecided on whether or not to take the next step. I wanted to go to her and bring her into the room with me but I knew that would be a mistake, this had to be Greer's decision alone.

As my eyesight sharpened I saw she was dressed only in a thin robe that did nothing to hide her body from my hungry eyes, her long burnished red hair hung down her back in a glossy sheet and her emerald green eyes were wide and a little wary as she approached the bed and sat down beside me. She had the ability to take my breath away every time I saw her and my senses were assailed by her addicting scent.

I slowly pushed myself up until I was sitting and took her hand in mine but we didn't speak. She studied my face for a long moment and then she stood up slowly untied her robe and slipped it from her shoulders, letting it fall in a pool on the floor. Completely naked and unadorned, she slid into bed beside me and I wrapped her in my arms as my cold dead heart began to beat erratically and the heat engulfed me. I was afraid to breathe...

Yvonne (Laurenson) Robertson was born on Holm in the beautiful Orkney Islands, off the north coast of Scotland. She married Neil in 1985 and with their two sons, lived in various locations in the UK including the tiny village of Glamis, the birthplace of the late Queen Elizabeth, the Queen Mother. Her son's, like all of the village children, spent many summers, playing in the beautiful castle grounds, now the home of the current Lord and Lady Strathmore.

In 2007 they made the momentous decision to immigrate to the US, where the idea to write a transatlantic love affair was born.

An avid poetry and short story writer most of her life she turned her hand to writing a romance novel and The Cuckoo In The Nest series was born, followed shortly afterward by the Vampire Brides series and the standalone book Craving The Love Of A Vampire Queen.

You can contact her on her website yvonnerobertsonauthor.com
Or by email yvonnerobertsonauthor@gmail.com

To submit a manuscript for our review,

email us at

submissions@majorkeypublishing.com

Major Key Publishing is accepting submissions from experienced & aspiring authors in the areas of Contemporary Romance, Urban Fiction, Paranormal, Mystery & Suspense & New Adult Romance!

If interested in joining a successful, independent publishing company, send the first 3-5 chapters of your completed manuscript to submissions@majorkeypublishing.com

Submissions should be sent as a Microsoft Word document, along with your synopsis and contact information.

WWW.MAJORKEYPUBLISHING.COM

Be sure to LIKE our Major Key Publishing page on Facebook!

Printed in Great Britain
by Amazon

43483285R00137